SACRED SHADOWS

SACRED SHADOWS

MAXINE ROSE SCHUR

DIAL BOOKS

New York

Published by Dial Books
A Division of Penguin Books USA Inc.
375 Hudson Street
New York, New York 10014

Copyright © 1997 by Maxine Rose Schur
All rights reserved
Designed by Ann Finnell
Printed in the U.S.A. on acid-free paper
First Edition
1 3 5 7 9 10 8 6 4 2

Library of Congress Cataloging in Publication Data
Schur, Maxine.
Sacred shadows / by Maxine Rose Schur.—1st ed.
p. cm.
Summary: When her German hometown becomes
part of Poland after World War I, Lena, a young
German Jew, struggles to come to terms with the anti-Semitism
and anti-German hatred that seems to be growing around her.
ISBN 0-8037-2295-8 (Tr.)
1. Jews—Poland—Juvenile fiction. [1. Jews—Poland—Fiction.
2. Prejudices—Fiction. 3. Poland—History—1918–1945—Fiction.] I. Title.
CuRR PZ7.S3964Sag 1997 [Fic]—dc21 97-5037 CIP AC

A great many incidents in this book are based on true events.
However, nearly all of the characters are fictional,
as is the town.—Maxine Rose Schur

For Ruth Wolff, my mother,
with love

I am indebted to Joanne Baumgart
and her sister, the late Thea Rostock,
for sharing their memories
of Poland with me.
I am forever grateful.

Are not even the rocks crowned with sacred shadows?

Does not the harvest yet ripen?

Does not a green countryside of bushes

and fields lie along the river?

And does not the wondrous arch of heaven still rise?

from Trilogy of Passion
Johann Wolfgang von Goethe

Ledniezno, Poland
March 1, 1932

I opened the door of our shoe store and looked far down the street. No photographer. Good. Clutching the parcel tightly, I stepped out. The air felt blade sharp, as it does just before a snowfall. I walked quickly, rehearsing my speech to Frau Gerhardt. I practiced constructing my words, pacing them and giving them just the right emphasis so their truth would be obvious to her.

When I reached the big house, I climbed the steps to the front door and used the brass knocker. Their maid, Hedwig, opened the door. Though I was twenty now, I could tell from her eyes she recognized me.

"I have brought shoes for Frau Gerhardt to try on," I told her. The maid stared at me coldly, but I quickly added, "Frau Gerhardt asked me to bring them."

"Use the trade entrance next time," she snapped as she led me across the polished floor of the hallway to the good room. When she left to call Frau Gerhardt, I looked about. Everything had changed since I'd spent so many happy hours in this room. Yet the room was unchanged.

The blue settee, where Dora and I had years ago lined up our dolls, still looked like new. The gray finch in the silver cage seemed some close descendant of the tiny bird Dora and I had taught to walk on our fingers. The Persian rug was soft as ever underfoot, and the steam heater still gurgled like a baby. Best of all, just as before, over the mantel hung the oil painting of the Rhine steamboat. This painting had been my very favorite thing in Dora's house. I would often stare at the scene until I felt as if I had actually entered its world. Now once again I looked at it closely. The Alps were frosted with snow that would never melt. Soundlessly the lacy boat traveled, the painted water forever disturbed by its movement. Now, more than ever, I wished I could escape into the painting and become one of its tiny, eternal passengers.

"So, Lena, you are here."

I turned quickly from the painting to see the mistress of the house. I curtsied. "Good morning, Frau Gerhardt. I brought you the evening shoes you wanted. They just arrived," I lied.

"Give them to me."

I handed the shoes to her, and she slipped off her pretty needlepoint slippers to put them on. Her beautiful legs were white as peeled horseradish, and the silk stockings she wore made them glimmer a fine pearl color. Her feet were small as a child's.

Frau Gerhardt walked slowly across the carpet, her slim figure youthful in her stylish green dress. When she reached the ebony piano, she kicked her leg up like a prancing horse and admired the silky blue of the shoe on her dainty foot.

"Are they truly from Feinstag's?" she inquired.

"Yes, Frau Gerhardt. We received a new shipment from Berlin last week."

"And they filled your order just like that?" she asked, arching her cinema-star eyebrows. "The order of Jews?"

"Yes," I lied again. "We have good credit with Feinstag's; we've dealt with them for years."

"What size are these?"

"Thirty-two. Exactly what you asked for."

Frau Gerhardt looked at the shoes for a long moment, and I knew she fancied them. Perhaps it is now, I thought, that I should say the words to her. The words I promised Mother I would say. I reached into the pocket of my coat and withdrew the little box. For I wanted to believe that when Frau Gerhardt, who had once liked me, would hear my words and see, actually see what was in the little box, she would change back again. She would understand and be good to Mother and me again. Yes, I wanted to believe that what was in the little box had this power.

ONE

Ledniesen, Germany
April 14, 1917

When I was told my father was dead, I ran away. I was at my friend Dora's house, and it was her mother who came into the good room as we dressed our dolls. Her eyes wet with tears, Frau Gerhardt cooed, "Lena dear, you must come with me, poor lamb. Your Ta Ta is dead. I must take you home, darling!" But I did not go with Dora's mother. I ran past her and straight out of the house. Across Geermacht Street, through the market square, and down Bierkaut Road. I was five years old and could run like the wind. I stopped for nothing, so even when I passed my teacher, Frau Hoffelmeyer, I neither curtsied nor said, "God punish England!" I flew as fast as I could, and when I got to City Park, I kept running until I reached the pine grove, and there

I flung myself down, hugged the damp earth, and waited.

I must have been there a long time and gotten very cold, for I remember how warm my brother's hands felt as he pulled me up from the ground. "Lena, get up!" he cried. "Look at you, all dirty!" Günther was twelve, but his voice was older, as if it were announcing in some way the grown-up he was to be. "Frau Hoffelmeyer saw you running like the devil. Why are you lying on the ground at a time like this!"

"I'm waiting for Ta Ta," I answered.

Günther pushed his brown curls back from his forehead and, with a low, flat voice, said, "Lena, Ta Ta is dead. Mother got a telegram. It said he was killed in France." Then Günther's voice grew very, very quiet, and he added softly, "Ta Ta is in Heaven."

"NO!" I shouted. "Mother said when people die, they go into the ground." I pointed to the earth. "Ta Ta is *here!*"

For a moment Günther looked as if he were going to explain life and death to me or the whereabouts of France or Heaven, but instead he took my muddy hand and, gripping it tightly, led me home.

———

"Lord, be merciful! May Wilhelm Katz enter your radiant paradise! Oh, heavenly Father! May he enter!" My aunt, Tante Ilse, cried so loudly that I could hear her wailing as Günther and I went up the steps to our house. Tante Ilse was standing in the kitchen stirring a pot of potato soup. Her round face, usually white as a plate, was now red, and every minute she blew her nose into a large blue handkerchief, the kind servant girls use.

When she saw me standing on the clean black-and-white tile floor, my cotton dress stained with dirt, my shoes and stockings caked with mud, and my brown curls stuck with leaves, my aunt let out a scream, then pulled me into the bathroom. She mixed Schwartzkopf powder with water and washed my hair and body vigorously, as if by scrubbing away dirt, she could scrub away grief.

Though they were sisters, Tante Ilse and my mother were as different as salt and pepper. My aunt was a highly emotional person, and though I loved her, the unpredictable weather of her moods scared me. "There!" she declared, after she had combed my damp hair and dressed me in a pinafore. "*Now* you look like my well-behaved niece. Stay clean and quiet in the good room until your poor mother comes home."

We Germans called the parlor the good room, but I didn't want to sit there. So instead, I went to my favorite place: the balcony. From the balcony, high over Giese Street, I could look far over our town. In one direction I could see all the way down to my school, and in the other all the way up to the Cathedral of Saint Adalbertus. The balcony's ornate black iron railing was bright with the red geraniums Ta Ta always fussed over. Every evening at seven I'd lean over the railing to watch for Mother and Günther, and before the war Father too, walking home from the shoe store.

Now, quiet and fearful, I stood on the balcony and

waited until I saw a carriage pull up in front of our house. After several moments Mother stepped down, her tall figure supported by my aunt, who had flown downstairs to meet her. The plump little woman brought Mother up the steps slowly, as if Mother were a hundred years old. When I went back into the good room, I saw Mother enter. She moved slowly, *strangely*. She did not walk so much as wade across the room, as a bather gradually enters the cold water of Lake Lipówka.

"Mother!" I cried in horror at this strange behavior. "Mother!" At my outburst she grabbed me and hugged me so hard, I feared my bones would break.

Günther hung back. But when Mother finally released me, she pulled him to her with the same awful fierceness.

Then I knew that whatever had happened to my father, what had happened to my mother was far more terrible. I began to wail.

My cries were like an alarm that set off commotion. At once Mother collapsed weeping into the brown velvet armchair. "Shaa!" Tante Ilse cried to me in great distress. "You're upsetting your dear mother!" But I paid no attention to my aunt and bawled even louder. Tante Ilse flew uselessly back and forth between Mother and me, trying to calm us both until at last she too succumbed, dropping suddenly like a shot bird onto the highback settee. We were all drowning in noisy sorrow except for Günther, who suddenly called from the balcony, "Mother, there's a coach out front . . . from the artillery garrison!"

In moments there came a knock at our door, and Mother, roused by the word *garrison*, wiped her eyes. Tante Ilse opened the door and a tall young soldier entered. His German uniform sparkled with brass buttons and his black boots gleamed like glass. I stopped crying to stare at him.

"Frau Katz?" he asked Tante Ilse. She shook her head, pointing to my mother. Then this handsome soldier stood before Mother, clicked his heels twice, and bowed in much magnified respect.

"Honorable Frau Katz," he intoned. "Sacrificing daughter of Germany. It is with the greatest regret we have received the news of the death of Cannoneer Captain Wilhelm Katz. . . ."

I didn't understand half of what the soldier said after that, yet his manner puzzled me more than his talk, for he didn't seem sad. On the contrary, as he spoke there came into his voice a ringing joy. He strode up and down our good room talking gloriously. The soldier's strong steps made the teacups tremble in our china cabinet, and under the rose rug the wood floor sighed. As he paced from the china cabinet to the window and back again, he spoke of my father, and his memorized speech was given with an authority even greater than a teacher's.

"Captain Katz laid down his life for the Fatherland!" he declared. "The great courage of this cannoneer leaves for all Germans an immortal song of heroism and sacrifice. Captain Katz was a soldier of the Kaiser and is now an eternal son of Germany!"

The soldier talked like this for a good while. Then

at last, to top off his wondrous words, he stopped and with practiced formality handed my mother a small box, bowed low as a servant, clicked his heels, and was gone.

After he left, Tante Ilse made Mother go upstairs to her bedroom; then she returned, sniffling, to the kitchen. She served Günther and me supper, mumbling piteously all the while we ate in silence. Then, after looking in on Mother, Tante Ilse lay down on our settee and quickly fell asleep. Günther went to his room. Scared by all the things I did not understand, I opened Günther's door. His back was turned to me as he lay on the floor leafing through his boy magazines. "Don't talk," he warned immediately. "Don't say anything—and close the door!"

Had everyone forgotten me? For the first night in my life I had to put myself to bed, and the very idea frightened me. Our family had recently installed electricity, so in my bedroom a lamp hung from the middle of the high ceiling. To turn it out, I would have had to push my chair under it, climb up, and pull the string my father had attached. I had never done this, because the trip back to bed in the blackness scared me too much. Each night as I lay safely in bed with my doll, Eva, Mother would come in to turn out the light. Now, too frightened to make the dark trip by myself, I left the light on, said my prayers, and slipped into bed, pressing my soft cheek against Eva's hard one.

But I could not sleep, for Ta Ta crowded my mind. Ta Ta's face warm and slightly scratchy when he kissed me good night. Ta Ta's deep laughter at my riddles and his somber voice singing the holy songs of Shabbos. I became more and more troubled by the confusion of what had happened to my father. My child question grew larger and larger until, unable to bear the uncertainty any longer, I began to cry.

I heard my door open. "Mother!" I shouted, springing up in bed. "Mother!" But it was not my mother; it was Günther, so I shot my question at him with all my heart:

"Günther," I cried, "is Ta Ta *very* dead?"

Günther did not answer me right away but came and sat on my bed. I knew by looking at his face he held the dark answer.

"Yes," he said at last. "Ta Ta is very dead. We'll not see him again. That's what dead is. That's what dead means."

His words struck me with a force I wasn't prepared to receive. "*I* will see Ta Ta again!" I declared ferociously.

Günther took both my hands in his and said gently, "No, Lena, you won't."

I looked into Günther's brown eyes. "Not ever?" I asked in a holy whisper. "Not even on my birthday?"

"Not even on your birthday."

And so it was that evening, in the brightness of my electric-lit room, that I began to learn the foreverness of death. I wept, for now my heart felt small and cold as a pebble.

Günther sat quietly while I sobbed. Then suddenly he reached into his pocket and pulled out the gray leather box I had seen the soldier give Mother. "Do you know what's in here?" he asked. But without waiting for me to answer, he said, "Of course you don't, so if you stop crying I'll show you."

As I gradually stopped crying, Günther pulled a wrinkled handkerchief from his pocket and I blew my nose. Then he opened the box and showed me a beautiful piece of jewelry. It was a silver leaf from which hung two tiny silver swords and beneath them a large black enamel cross. The lovely pin was topped by a glossy red-black-and-white-striped ribbon tied into a perfect bow.

"Will Mother wear that brooch on her coat?" I asked.

"No, goosey. It's not a brooch. It's a medal. It's the Iron Cross, a military honor that was awarded to Ta Ta for his great bravery in the war. It means"—and here Günther's voice was very solemn—"that Ta Ta is a hero, a martyr for our Fatherland."

I didn't know what a martyr was or what heroes did exactly, but I understood bravery and that sounded good.

Günther spoke much like the soldier. He told me that Ta Ta had fought in a great battle at a place in France called Verdun. He said that Ta Ta and thousands of other men had at first brilliantly captured much land from the French, but then a few weeks ago the French had beaten the Germans back, and the gallant but outnumbered Germans had been defeated. Ta Ta's bravery at Verdun had earned him great respect and would be remembered, perhaps even brought to the attention of Field Marshal von Hindenburg. "Our father's honor is eternal," Günther told me.

I did not understand then all of what Günther said. But that didn't matter, for it was Günther's manner more than his words that soothed me. I sensed that if Günther, who skied with Ta Ta every winter—Günther, who worked so closely with him in the shoe store after school—Günther, who at night read with him the books of Moses Mendelssohn—if Günther, who loved Ta Ta as much as I did, was not sorrowful, then things would be fine. With great conviction Günther spoke to me of Ta Ta's veneration in Heaven, and except for a slight trembling of his lower lip, Günther did not appear grieved.

"And Heaven is very nice, isn't it?" I asked.

"It's the nicest place there is," he answered simply. Then, seeing that I was now sleepy, Günther kissed my cheek as Ta Ta used to do, turned off the light, and left. I fell asleep hugging Eva, only dimly aware later of the muffled sobs from my brother's room.

TWO

When I returned to school the next week, Frau Hoffelmeyer made a fuss about my father. Dabbing her wrinkly eyes with the hankie she kept tucked under her watch, she intoned, "The memory of Captain Katz is one of duty and glory forever cherished in our Fatherland!" Other girls in the school had a dead father, a wounded uncle, a missing brother, yet I must admit that for a good while after my father died, I took a conceited pride in my loss. I felt touched with honor myself by his death, and somehow my pride lessened my pain.

As the months passed, Frau Hoffelmeyer followed the war with an increased passion. Every morning after we sang the German national anthem, she would yank down the wall map of Europe and rap it hard with her pointer. "Today we are making a vigorous attack on the Somme!" she would sing, or "Girls, south of the Marne we've executed a terrific bombardment!"

Around the walls of our classroom Frau Hoffelmeyer had pinned up portraits of the top German commanders cut from the newspaper. When she felt particularly aggressive in her patriotism, she would, without warning, pick one of us to quiz on their names. This was difficult, for there were twelve of them, like the gods of Mount Olympus, and they all wore the same uniforms and the same big mustaches, and generally looked alike.

I always did poorly, for even if I remembered the name, I would not know the rank, like the time I knew the picture was Ludendorff's but nothing more.

"Lena, stand up and identify this glorious soldier."

"It is Colonel Ludendorff," I answered.

SLAP! Frau Hoffelmeyer's large hand smacked my face. This was the cue to answer again.

"It is Major Ludendorff," I said with no confidence.

At this answer Frau Hoffelmeyer looked especially offended, as if some affront had been made to one of her family.

SLAP!

"It is Admiral Ludendorff," I peeped.

SLAP!

Seeing that I had run out of my inadequate list of ranks, Frau Hoffelmeyer turned her aged, military face to the class. "Girls," she proclaimed, "this glorious soldier is *General* Ludendorff. Repeat five times."

While my face burned red, the other girls sprang to their feet, chanting: "General Ludendorff! General Ludendorff! General Ludendorff! General Ludendorff! General Ludendorff!"

Frau Hoffelmeyer's slaps felt like little explosions that left my teeth aching for days, yet I never once cried, for I did not think them cruel. This was the way we learned all our subjects—a slap for each wrong answer. It was the way all teachers taught.

And, of course, like all teachers at that time, Frau Hoffelmeyer kept a "prayer pot." It worked like this: When the teacher entered the class, the custom was for children to rise, curtsy, and say, "Good morning." But now, during the war, we had to say instead, "God punish England!" If by mistake a girl said, "Good morning," she'd have to pay a five-pfennig fine. On the streets too we were expected to curtsy and say, "God punish England!" when meeting a grown-up. If a girl forgot to say it, her omission would be reported to the school, and she would pay five pfennigs. All the pfennigs were put into the prayer pot, formerly a pickle jar. At the end of the year, Frau Hoffelmeyer said, we would use the pfennigs to buy canned meat to send to the glorious soldiers. The prayer pot was to teach us to keep a German victory uppermost in our minds, for as Frau Hoffelmeyer often reminded us, "The war is the very most sacred thing."

Like religion, the war entered every part of our life. In synagogue on Friday evenings Rabbi Fried led us in prayer for German victory. After services I'd sit in the sanctuary with my mother and other ladies as they cut, rolled, and packed cotton bandages for the front.

And in the streets, war was everywhere, from our jump-rope songs—

"Jump for glory or you'll be sorry!"
"Jump for winning or you'll be sinning!"
"Jump for the Kaiser for the Kaiser's wiser!"
"Jump for Germany, THE BEST IN THE WORLD!"

to the newsboys' shouts—

"GERMANY SET TO WIN FREEDOM OF THE
  SEAS!"
"LUDENDORFF OFFENSIVE GREAT SUCCESS!"
"GERMANY PREPARES FOR VICTORY!"

Ledniesen was a garrison town, so it was common to see the large military coaches roll through our old, narrow streets. Sometimes too we'd see the new horseless army trucks heading to the front. I remember being afraid of them, for it seemed to me their engines sounded the very groan and boom of battle itself.

Yet it was home where we most felt the war. The war had taken not only our father but also our daily life as we had known it. Mother now worked longer hours in the shoe store. In her brief time at home she did all the cleaning and cooking, though with our German farmers gone to war, there was little to cook. We had some money, but food was so scarce, money or not, we all were forced to eat what was previously given to cattle: beets and fodder corn. To feed the cattle, we were asked to save coffee grounds, fruit pits, pinecones, and green leaves, which we gave weekly to Flinker, the ragman, to deliver to the farms. Having no flour for bread, we made large round crackers from ground fodder corn.

By autumn Mother ripped out Ta Ta's geraniums and sowed carrots in the planter boxes. We ate wild mushrooms and collected the gummy chestnuts that fell in the synagogue yard. By the spring of 1918 everyone in Ledniesen ate whatever they could find; some people even boiled weeds. By that time ration cards for bread, milk, sugar, vegetables, and meat were useless. There was no bread, no milk, no sugar, no vegetables, no meat.

Then suddenly, in November 1918, the war was over. We had lost the war and, as the newspapers told us, nearly two million of our men. Nearly two million! And though defeat was a terrible shock, I remember Mother saying that despite the great losses, we could now begin to live normal lives. In November, too, we learned the men would be coming home. On special trains from France and Belgium.

One afternoon, the week after my seventh birthday, Dora and I were playing in the stockroom of the shoe store. Though her house was grand, with the loveliest of toys, she preferred to play here among the floor-to-ceiling shelves of shoe boxes. Here there were dark hiding places and no tattletale maids. Here there were shoe boxes for doll beds and great stacks of pink tissue paper for the coverlets. Here were long shoelaces for the sewing cards we cut from the shoe box covers. Here were old labels that served as make-believe ration cards and metal shoehorns for flipping marbles. And best of all, here were last year's fashion catalogues from Berlin showing beautiful people we could cut out for paper dolls.

On this afternoon Dora and I were gluing these paper dolls to cardboard so they could stand. Suddenly we heard a distant sound of music.

"Just Gypsies," said Dora.

"Doesn't sound like Gypsies," I said. "Sounds bigger . . . like a band!"

We ran to the front of the shop. Mother and Günther had opened the door and were looking far down the street. Our customers hurried shoeless to the window. Dora and I dashed outside. At first we could see nothing, just a blur of figures in the distance. Then the music grew louder and we saw them! Hundreds of men in uniform and walking up Bierkaut Road. People emptied out of the shops, mingling with the people on the street, quickly forming a cheering crowd. As the men came closer, people went wild. "God's blessed!" shouted a woman, and then the cry went up, *"Sieg! Sieg! Sieg!"* "Victory! Victory! Victory!"

Dora and I squeezed through the crowd of grownups and took a good viewing position right in front. I did not understand what I saw. First I saw a small group of soldiers walking while playing instruments. They were followed by what looked like a parade of beggars. They were soldiers such as I had never seen, ragged and sickly. Many were thin as corpses and crippled. A few looked not much older than Günther but wore the faces of old men. One of these younger ones walked like a marionette! Another, a tall fellow, walked quickly, but his useless arm swung from side to side like the pendulum on our grandfather clock. "Martyrs!" an old woman shouted, and soon the chant was taken up. "Martyrs! Martyrs! Martyrs!" A dog barked at the men and was given a swift kick. I saw Herr Glauptman, the owner of the stationery shop, weep openly. Some people pressed coins into the hands of the most wounded. The music was drowned by the emotional cries of the crowd. The soldiers kept coming. Some of them had faces still as death. Then I saw a man who seemed to be missing a face!

I screamed and turned to run back into our store, but Dora grabbed my arm. "Lena," she cried excitedly. "Stay! Look, here they are! Just as we learned. Look! Our glorious soldiers!"

THREE

Ledniezno, Poland
November 1918–January 1919

One morning in November of 1918 I woke up in my own room but found myself in a different country. I heard a wild sort of singing, jumped out of bed, and ran to the front balcony. In both directions as far as I could see marched crowds of singing people. Many of them carried what looked like the German flag, except it was red and the eagle white instead of black.

"Lena, don't stand there. Come inside."

I turned to see my mother, still in her nightclothes, hair down to her waist.

"Mother! Why aren't you dressed?"

"Come inside and I'll tell you."

I went in and sat at our kitchen table as Mother prepared our breakfast. But still she didn't explain.

At last I asked, "Aren't you going to the shoe store this morning?"

"No, not today. It's not safe. As you see, the streets are full of ruffians." She sat down at the table and, concealing her emotions, said, "Lena, we don't live in Germany anymore. This is no longer our Fatherland. We are now living in Poland."

"Poland!" I looked at Mother in shock. "How can this be Poland when it's Germany!"

Then, patiently and as would fit a seven-year-old mind, Mother explained to me how once, nearly 125 years earlier, there had been a country called Poland, but through wars it got carved up like a New Year's goose. Part of it became Russian, part Austrian, and where we lived, in the province of Poznań—German.

"Why can't it just *stay* German?" I asked.

"Because," Mother explained, "when we lost the war, President Wilson of the United States made Germany agree to many things, and one of them was that all former Polish land is to be given back to Poland. So now for the first time since 1795 Poland will again be a country. That is why the Poles are celebrating."

She sat down at the table, served herself coffee from the copper pot, and poured a little into my cup. She spread our rye bread with a drop of chicken fat, and as we ate I plied Mother with questions. Would everyone speak Polish now? Would we have to salute the Polish flag? Would Polish girls come into our German school? Would my spelling tests be in Polish?

"I don't have answers," she said. "None of us know what will happen, but we must have faith that everything will work out." That was often her answer to me. She was a strong, steady woman and had a stubborn belief that eventually things right themselves.

Weeks passed, but still I wasn't allowed out of the house. Polish independence had let loose a wave of rage. Every single one of our 80,000 German soldiers left, and as they went, they looted Polish shops. In revenge, bands of Poles attacked Germans. They tore down German street signs, ripped up German flags, then trampled them in the mud. Our Governor General, Herr Beseler, was the first to flee into Germany, and with him went thousands of German families.

In less than a month all that was left to remind anyone that this had once been Germany was ourselves, the small number of Germans who stayed behind. But we dared not go out. We were scared of these wild Polish nationalists. Günther begged Mother to let us go to Germany. "We are German citizens," he kept saying. "Germans should live in Germany!"

"Let's wait and see" was all Mother replied. What was she thinking? One afternoon in early January, when Tante Ilse came to visit, we knew.

That afternoon Mother and I were sitting on the settee in the good room. Because my German school was closed during the riots, each afternoon Mother taught me herself—spelling, arithmetic, and sewing. She was teaching me to hem a handkerchief when we heard a knocking at the door. Opening it, I saw Tante Ilse. "Good afternoon, Auntie," I said curtsying. She kissed me absentmindedly and hurried into the good room. As usual she was in a flutter, but that day she was more agitated than usual. Her hat was lopsided and her coat buttoned wrong. We looked at her in surprise. Tante Ilse stood in front of my mother, caught her breath, then said with importance:

"Gisela, I have news for you."

"I have news too," Mother said quietly. "Take off your coat and sit down. Lena, bring your aunt some coffee."

I brought her the coffee, but when Tante Ilse took it, her hand trembled and she put the cup and saucer down on the side table, then announced in a great rush, "I am going to Germany. I don't want to leave you and the children alone, but I cannot stay here. If this land is no longer Germany, then I no longer belong on it. After all, we are safe only as citizens in our own country."

Having said her words, Tante Ilse seemed to grow calmer. She took up her coffee and drank deeply.

I could see Mother was thinking before replying. After a moment's silence she said, "I wish you well. Of course, Ilse, I wish you would stay, for we will miss you. And I agree with you that Germany is our Fatherland. Yet I wonder whether you've really considered your move. If you read the *Berliner Tageblatt* you'll see things are very unsettled in Germany. There is no more Kaiser, so who is running the country? No one. Germany is in chaos. Unemployment, workers on strike, and poverty. Terrible poverty! We Germans are in debt to every country we fought. Germany is unsettled—more unsettled than Poland."

"Germany more unsettled than Poland!" Tante Ilse

cried. "You're as wrong as if you'd eaten your hat! Can't you hear the criminals in the street? Can't you see the masses of poor people pouring in from the former Russian areas? And they bring more than lice! Remember, they come from *Russia*. The guns of the revolution are still hot there, and these 'Russian Poles' will spread Communism here like influenza!"

"I don't believe it," Mother replied, resuming her sewing.

"Well *I* believe it," Tante Ilse cried. "What's more"—and here Tante Ilse made her voice low and deep, as she did whenever she felt she was playing her trump card—"Poles *hate* Jews."

At this Mother stiffened and glanced at me, then back to her sister. "Don't talk in this way in front of children, Ilse. It's not right."

"Right or not, it's true," my aunt insisted. "Your children know it anyway, don't you, Lena?"

I looked at my aunt but did not answer. It was true that sometimes children would shout at me, "Go back to Palestine!" and that Günther had been in fistfights with Polish boys. Yet at my aunt's question I remained silent, for fear that if I agreed with her, I'd somehow betray Mother.

"I have had polite relationships with many of my Polish customers," Mother said. "We buy food from them; they buy shoes from us. They need our business. We need theirs. Of course there are Poles who dislike Jews, but I have faith that independence, with its new democratic Polish constitution, will make old prejudices quickly die."

"Well," Tante Ilse said, "I hope your faith pays off. But in my opinion you're too optimistic, or perhaps you haven't heard that in these weeks since independence, Poles have massacred Jews in Lwów and other towns. Is *this* the Poland in which you put your faith?"

Mother was going to respond to this, but Tante Ilse went right on. "As far as I'm concerned it's a foolish idea to stay. Here you are twice cursed. In your own country you'd be called the widow of a war hero, but here, Gisela, you are unwelcome as a German and unwelcome as a Jew."

Mother, who had remained calm throughout Tante Ilse's talk, now burst aflame with anger. "Shaa!" she hissed at her sister. "Stop this wicked talk! You exaggerate everything! Let me tell you *my* news first before you make your judgments!"

Mother put down her sewing and crossed the room to the oak desk. She opened the top right drawer, drew out an envelope, and handed it to Tante Ilse.

"Braunschweig's in Berlin?" Tante Ilse said, noting it was from the shoe store's main office. She took out the letter and read it aloud:

To All Braunschweig Branch Managers:

Because of the forthcoming closing of the Braunschweig stores in Poland, we are first offering each current manager the early opportunity of purchasing your branch store and its merchandise at a favorable price. If you are interested in this opportunity, please contact this office for further information. . . .

"You want to *buy* the shoe store?" Tante Ilse asked Mother in amazement. "With what money?"

"Wilhelm and I saved a little money," Mother said quietly, "and though my widow's pension is small, it might help me to purchase the store. Here God is giving me the chance to own my own store. In Germany, Ilse, I would not have this chance."

"What about holding on to the store? Braunschweig's may sell you the store, but the land it's on is now Polish, and the Poles will not let you succeed. They'll drive you out of business."

"I will succeed," Mother said, her strong face animated by her belief. "With patience you'll see many things change. At the Paris Peace Conference, President Wilson is making Poland pledge to protect its minorities. The Peace Treaty contains two articles just to protect the Jews! The words guaranteeing our rights will be right there—right in the treaty! You'll see, with the war over, life will improve for Jews here and throughout Europe. Because from now on, Ilse, the whole world is watching."

FOUR

Tante Ilse moved to Germany. She settled in a suburb of Berlin and eventually found work as a dressmaker. Mother bought the shoe store and from the beginning we all worked in it. Mother managed the store and waited on customers. Günther kept the accounts, and I—well, I didn't do anything at first except play, but by the time I was nine, I could dust, sweep, and fetch shoes from the back room by their inventory number. And it was a grand thing to work in the shoe store, for when Mother bought it, she changed it so dramatically that people from as far away as Danzig came to buy from us. It was not just the beauty of the carpet and wallpaper that drew people; it was the shoes

Mother imported from Berlin, Paris, and Milan. Elegant shoes in the latest fashions. In the window she cleverly draped empty shoe crates with green velvet and placed on them the smallest-sized ladies' shoes. There they perched prettily, and how they drew people in! Frau Gerhardt with her Frankfurt friends arriving in motorcars and draped in furs. Old women with feet lumpy as root vegetables. Shy soldiers accompanying their girlfriends. Farmers with the smell of the barn on them and their wives with feet long as butter paddles. Finicky brides cramming their toes into satin pumps, and children skating around and around our carpet on slippery new soles. It was a profitable amusement.

The hard years seemed behind us, for my father's death and the privations of war grew dim. I was happy in my child world, but Günther, now nineteen, was unhappy. Every day he spoke of Germany. He talked of the big cities—Berlin, Hamburg, Frankfurt—of their universities and all they could offer him. Mother said that in a few years we might go live in our Fatherland, but Günther did not want to wait.

"Life for Jews here has gotten no better!" he argued. "I can't be a lawyer, a journalist, or even a postman! Why? Because I am a Jew!"

"The government will change" was Mother's simple answer. "And in the meantime we have the store to care for. You'll manage the store one day."

"I don't want to manage a store," Günther said softly. "I want to write."

In October of 1924, when I was twelve, Günther, tall as a man but dear as a boy, kissed Mother and me good-bye. He was off to Berlin to study journalism.

One evening, a week after Günther left, Mother and I were walking home from work. In the dimming light Mother was silent, perhaps sobered by the realization our little family had grown yet smaller. Above us the pink sky glowed, and the bells of Saint Adalbertus tolled the hour. As we went, the warm smell of pork stew drifted from the noisy restaurants where soldiers ate with their girls. We passed two priests and then a group of Hasidic Jews in long black coats and round fur hats big as automobile wheels. When we turned onto our street, I said shyly, "Mother, I will be thirteen next month but never have had a birthday party." Mother had little liking for parties, for she was so serious, yet at my question she stopped and looked at me.

"Please, Mother," I said, "just a small one . . . just six of us . . . not a real party even . . . no boys . . . just a gathering."

"Whom would you invite?" she asked. "All the girls in your class?" My school, the Higher German Daughters' School, was now so small that my class had only six pupils.

"Yes," I answered, "only the five other girls in my class."

"If you want this party, you will have it." Mother said emphatically. "I will bake a Black Forest cake for you, and we'll make buttermilk. Pick the date and then you can tell your friends."

I was overjoyed at Mother's ready acceptance, but I decided not to *tell* my friends. I had a better idea. A wonderful idea! That evening I pulled from under my bed the wooden boot box in which I kept my sewing things. Inside lay a large square of thin white cotton that I measured carefully, then cut into five smaller squares. I would hem these squares to make handkerchiefs and embroider each one with a different flower and the date of my party. These would be my friends' invitations and also their party souvenirs. And each flower would be unique, matching the personality of the girl.

On a piece of paper I started to sketch the flowers, and as I did, I thought about my girlfriends. I started with Thea. Though she was shy, she was kind and smart, always helping me with my homework. Her handkerchief would have a daisy, modest but cheerful. Then there was Greta, Jewish like me. Greta was chubby, her hair full of curls round and gold as coins. She was fun, for she always had a joke or a secret, but most important, she alone had an older sister and so knew the answers to life's mysteries. Sometimes Greta mocked our ignorant selves with her knowledge until we begged her to tell us what a "period" was and where babies *really* came from. Then she would educate us in such a theatrical way that we were sleepless for days. For Greta—a bright purple poppy.

Next I thought of Birgit. She was tall with skin the color of very light toast. She could yodel and swim, and her good-natured laugh was hearty as a boy's. For her I would embroider a sunflower. Then, of course, there was Dora—the center of our circle. For Dora, with her dark auburn hair and creamy skin, was the most lovely. Dora, with her grand house, elegant mother, rich clothes, and witty words was the star in our little group. And I, as her best friend, her almost-sister, was like her moon, reflecting a little radiance too, just from being so close to her. I would embroider a red rose for Dora. An elegant, cultivated flower and the most beautiful.

I looked at my choices and was pleased. But suddenly my heart sank as I remembered the other Jewish girl in our class—the new girl, Sala. I must invite her, I thought, though we did not consider Sala a friend. Well, who could be friends with someone so witless? Someone who always said such silly things. Like the first day we ever saw her, when she entered our classroom holding a huge book.

"What is that under your arm?" Herr Hirschberg asked.

And the stupid girl answered, "It is a book of songs by Felix Mendelssohn." If she had stopped there, she would have been smart; but no, she had to add, "He is my uncle." To think that someone as cunning as Herr Hirschberg would believe that the great German composer could be the uncle of a girl with straggly hair, a nose long as a flute, and a skirt like a Gypsy's. No wonder right then she was given three smacks on her palm for lying.

Sala always said ridiculous things. Once Dora asked teasingly, "Sala, don't you have a boyfriend?"

And she answered, "There's no wind today and no clouds at all!"

What could anyone make of that? Dora and Greta made much of it, for often when one of our group asked a question, the two would answer in mock dreaminess, "There's no wind today and no clouds at all!"

There was one thing I did like about Sala, though, and that was her singing. Most of the children in our school were Lutheran, which we called Evangelical. In the afternoon the Evangelical children sang their songs in a choir. The Jewish children could go home. But Sala, along with Greta and me, stayed to sing the songs too, for though the words did not match our religion, we loved the sacred music and the chance to be in a real choir. Because she was tall, Sala stood in the back, and when we sang *"Lass mich gehen,"* her voice floated above us, so in tune, it guided us like an accompanying instrument.

I looked at my embroidery threads. A chrysanthemum, that's what I would make for Sala. Tall. Shaggy. Detached.

It took me a week to make the invitations, and when I finished, I showed them to Mother. She examined them carefully, then said to me, "You are very good at this. You could be a skilled dressmaker someday." She gave me powder-blue envelopes with scalloped edges. I slipped a hankie-invitation into each envelope and the next day, in great excitement, brought them to school in my dress pocket, for I planned to hand them out at second breakfast.

Second breakfast was the light meal we took at eleven in the courtyard. The girls in my class always sat on the same two corner benches. That morning all the girls were there except Sala, who in her slowpoke way often arrived late. We each pulled out our bread-and-butter sandwiches, which we wrapped in the new style with waxed paper. We ate quickly, and when we finished, we all took the waxed paper, shook off the crumbs, and folded it along the same creases, for as it was expensive, we used it again and again. Only Dora threw hers away. I had planned at this very moment—after we folded our waxed paper—to hand out my invitations. So with great excitement I pulled from my pocket the blue envelopes.

"I have something for each of you," I announced happily. The reaction of my friends to both the invitations and the party was just what I wanted.

"Yours will be the first party I've ever been to in my entire life," cried Birgit. "I can't wait!"

"I adore parties," Greta declared, "even without boys!"

"Darling little handkerchief!" Thea cooed. "Do I really get to keep it?"

"I love the rose," Dora said. "It's my favorite flower. Oh, for the party, let's all do our hair in curls!"

While we were chattering in this way, I noticed Sala approach. Seeing that we were all squeezed on one bench with no room for her, she went to sit on the other bench, which was empty, and in her dreamy way unfolded her newspaper-wrapped bread.

"I swear," Dora whispered to us. "Sala never looks as if she's wearing clothes but *laundry*!" This observation struck us all as very funny, and we began to giggle.

I glanced at Sala and saw the wit in Dora's words. Sala had on a thin cardigan in the color of cooked cabbage. Underneath it she wore a blouse with a frayed lace collar. The blouse was too small for her and wouldn't stay tucked into her skirt. And what a skirt! To the ankles! As none of us in 1924 would have dreamed of wearing. Dora is right, I thought. She *is* a ridiculous sight. Sala, aware that I was watching her, looked up from her food, and for a moment our eyes met. She smiled, but I looked away.

"Come," I said to my friends, "let's walk back to class."

And as we passed Sala, I reached my hand into my pocket and felt her invitation. But I never took it out.

FIVE

For days before my party I was in a flutter. Perhaps it was silly to make such a fuss over just four friends and not one of them even a boy, but because it was my first party, I wanted everything to be nice. Besides the Black Forest cake Mother baked, I made tiny black-bread sandwiches of egg, cheese, and smoked carp and helped Mother make buttermilk. Loveliest of all, I took Mother's little cut-glass bowls out of the china cabinet and piled them with bittersweet choco-lates, each tucked in its own nest of red paper. The buttercups I had gathered in the synagogue yard I stuck in jars that I placed all about the good room. And on the table, which Mother had let me set with the linen tablecloth and serviettes embroidered with

Gothic K's, I set out place cards that I had drawn with buttercups to match.

An hour before my party, Mother curled my short brown hair with the tongs, and I put on my dress. It wasn't a party dress, for as much as I pleaded, Mother was set against the wastefulness of a party dress. "There's no point in spending money on a dress that you'll wear twice, then outgrow." So I wore my long-sleeved, knee-length cotton dress in navy blue with the wide white sash around the hips. In *Das Fräulein* magazine I had seen the charming effect of tucking a sprig of roses at the side of a hip sash, so I tucked some buttercups into the sash, and Mother pronounced this look "chic."

At two, when the knock came at the door, I flew to it. The four girls tumbled in, hair in curls and dressed like dolls. Greta wore a dress of pale blue crepe de Chine that she had sneaked out of her sister's wardrobe. The style was too grown-up for her, for it was flat and loose where a bust should have been yet, because of her plumpness, tight everywhere else. Thea wore a party dress in green and white georgette and sported an enormous green georgette bow in her hair. Birgit wore a cotton dress like mine in yellow, but it was already too short for her. And Dora! She was wearing a drop-waist party dress of strawberry-colored satin, and she was wearing silk stockings! We all wore wool stockings, and our mothers dressed up in cotton stockings. But now Dora had on the new silk stockings that only our richest lady customers wore. We took turns feeling Dora's silk-lined calves and listening to the grown-up whispers they made when she rubbed them ever so slightly together.

We were all hungry, so we sat at the table and fell upon the sandwiches at once. At first we tried to observe ladylike party manners. We ate the sandwiches with delicate pinched fingers and said *"Bitte"* and *"Danke."* But as we ate, we grew back into ourselves. I poured glasses and glasses of buttermilk, and we talked excitedly, reaching across each other for sandwiches, laughing with our mouths full.

"What shall we do next?" I asked the girls when we had finished.

"Oh, you must open your presents now," Birgit said. "Presents always come after food."

This was just what I wanted to do and was glad Birgit suggested it. As a way of thanks, I opened her gift first: a set of colored crayons, forty of them in their own gray metal box.

"Well, you're always doodling dresses in class when Herr Hirschberg isn't watching. Now you can color them," Birgit said.

"Great! I'll design a hat and dress for you, Birgit, with matching shoes, of course."

Thea's gift was a book of poetry by the great German poet Johann von Goethe. "The poems are so romantic," said Thea, "they'll make you cry!"

Dora's gift was exquisite: a small cloche hat in dove gray encircled by a mauve silk ribbon. "Dora!" I squealed. "It's the most beautiful hat ever!"

"I hope you like my present," said Greta. "I chose it

myself." Rose-scented toilet water from Cologne in a bottle shaped like a rose! That was Greta's grown-up gift. "You must sprinkle some in your hair," Greta said knowingly. "Boys love it."

"All boys?" Dora asked.

"All boys," Greta answered.

"What else do they like?" Dora asked, and the room at once became silent as we hung on the answer.

Greta sighed and daintily smoothed the folds of her dress. Her face took on a dutiful look, as if it were her burden to explain God to a group of heathens. At last she said slowly, drawing out each word, "They like to kiss."

Birgit started to giggle and Dora slapped her arm. "Sssshhh!"

"What I don't understand," Dora said, "is how you know *when* they want to kiss."

"I suppose they just tell you," I said.

Greta gave me a withering look. "They don't *tell* you," she said. "They give clues."

"Tell us," we begged. "Tell us!"

"They say certain things," she said. " 'Mmmmm, your lips are a rosebud,' or 'Your eyes are stars.' "

"Oh," sighed Thea. "If a boy ever said anything like that to me, I'd faint from happiness!"

"If you fainted," said Greta, "you'd never get to kiss him. I heard my sister tell her friend that if you want to be kissed, you have to be ready."

Birgit started giggling again. She stuck her lips out in a silly way and made smacking sounds.

"You don't stick your lips out at all," I said, as if I knew. "When a girl kisses Rudolph Valentino, she doesn't do anything different with her lips."

"That's right," Greta said. "Don't make your mouth into a duckbill. Just close your eyes and tilt your head up!"

We all sighed.

"What's the point of knowing how to kiss if we'll never get a chance to do it?" Dora asked bitterly. It was true. Boys could not attend our school, so where could we find them? Where could we meet them?

"Leave honey on the plate—flies will come," Greta said, batting her eyelashes.

"What does that mean?" I asked.

"It means you have to *attract* boys if you want to meet them. You've got to talk with teasing in your voice. That's flirting. You've got to walk wiggly—as if you're walking to slow music. You've got to smell nice! You should wear cologne on your shoulders. Put Simon cream on your face and hands to keep your skin soft. And your cheeks should have a rosy blush."

"A rosy blush . . . a rosy blush." Thea repeated Greta's words as if they were holy. Greta meanwhile crossed over to the little side table and brought back a glass dish of chocolates.

"Now watch carefully," she ordered. She popped a chocolate into her mouth, then took its thin red wrapper and rubbed it gently on each cheek. "See?"

The red paper stained Greta's cheeks pink. We watched, amazed and delighted; then we each copied this trick ourselves. "Learned it from our servant girl," Greta said.

"We could wear rouge without our mothers ever knowing!" Birgit whispered.

"That's the point," sighed Greta.

"Still," Dora persisted, "to attract boys, there have to be boys to attract!"

Then methodically, as we'd done many times before, we went over the boys we knew. First we went over the handful of German ones, but they were either too old for us or too young or what Greta called "boring." Then we went over the Polish ones. We talked of the boys at the Polish school, but some of them didn't even speak German, and besides, they didn't like German girls. Many of them were handsome, but as Birgit said, "They're just too different." I thought of the Jewish boys who went to synagogue, only nine of them and not one even close to our age.

"When we're older," Greta said, "we can date soldiers from the garrisons. They're all about, and you can tell if one likes you if he teases you."

"You have to meet one before he can tease you," Thea said.

"Oh, soldiers are easy to meet!" Greta laughed. "They're like birds—you lure them with bread."

"You bake bread for them?" asked Birgit.

"Don't be ridiculous! You *trade* breads with them. They get garrison bread as their ration. But most of the fellows don't like the dark bread. So you walk past the garrison with a loaf of white bread, and when you see a good-looker, you ask him if he'd like to swap.

It's *the* way to start talking with them. All my sister's friends do it."

"My mother would never let me do that," Dora announced.

"Nor mine," I said.

"My mother," Greta announced, "once found my sister had bought a white bread and made her eat the whole loaf before she could leave the house!" For several moments there was silence as we pictured this.

"I suppose we'll just have to wait for your brother to come back!" Birgit teased me with a mock sigh.

"I wish there were more German boys here now," Thea said.

Dora crossed her legs like a grown lady and said, "In Germany there are millions of handsome boys. Millions! My mother says we will one day live in the Reich again . . . then I'll have my pick."

"Why doesn't your family move there now?" asked Birgit.

"Well," Dora said proudly, "you know how much land my father owns, but he says if he sold it now, the money he'd get would be worthless in Germany. My parents say we'll stay right here until Germany conquers this part of Poland again."

"Do you think that will really happen?" I asked.

"Of course!" Dora answered, looking astonished at my ignorance. Then, as if reciting a memorized line of poetry, she proclaimed, "Right now there are brave people in our Fatherland who are struggling to bring us the glory we deserve!"

"Is that what your parents say?" Thea asked.

"Yes, my parents and their friends say that one day the National People's Party will bring honor to Germany—honor that other people have taken away."

"What other people?" I asked.

Dora looked confused for a moment, then looked down. "I don't know," she answered quietly.

"Greta," Birgit said, "teach us how to do the Charleston!"

"Oh, it's easy!" Greta cried, jumping up and grabbing Birgit. "Look." She swung Birgit around. "Just copy what I do. Kick forward! Kick back! Swing forward! Swing back! Turn your toes in! Now out! In! Out! In! Out! Good! Make your knees knock. Slap your right knee! Slap your left! Slap your bottom! Spin around!" We laughed hysterically, and I grabbed Birgit. Dora grabbed Thea, and we all danced this crazy new dance while Greta sang in terrible English, "Charleston, Charleston, from Carolina!" Squealing and laughing, we pranced and shimmied all around the dining table. Round and round and round, falling over each other, smacking palm against palm, lifting our skirts, slapping our behinds, and showing our bloomers. "Charleston, Charleston, from Carolina!"

"Lena. Lena!" We froze to see my mother standing in the doorway.

Mother looked as if she were going to say something about frolicking in the house, but before she could, I said, "Mother, Greta has shown us how to do the new American dance!"

Mother smiled and winked at me. "I was going to bring in your cake."

I knew what the wink meant. Before the party—trying not to hurt her feelings—I'd asked Mother to not come into the good room. If I was going to have a party, I told her, it would be no fun with a mother hovering about, watching and listening. "I'll only come in once," she had promised, "to bring in the cake."

Now Mother brought in the cake topped with whipped cream and cherries. We sang, *"Ich freue mich, dass ich geboren bin und habe Geburtstag heute!"* "I am happy that I was born and my birthday is today!" I cut the slices myself, and we ate them all up. When we finished, I didn't want the party to be over. I had planned for us to play guessing games, but now I was too shy to suggest them, as I thought Dora might think games babyish. Birgit suggested we take a walk to City Park, but Greta didn't want to. Then Dora got an idea.

"You know," she said, linking her arm affectionately in mine, "since we're all good friends . . . we should make a Truth Circle."

"What's that?" I asked.

"Oh, it's not a game, really. It's more like a favor that friends can do for each other. We pick one girl. Then we all sit in a circle, and each of us must tell that girl a truth about herself. A truth that perhaps she doesn't see. We make her see herself realistically, then give her advice that's helpful."

"But what if what we say hurts the girl's feelings?" Thea asked.

"How could it?" Dora shot back. "None of us would say anything mean or untrue about each other, would we?"

"Of course we wouldn't!" Greta agreed. "But which one of us should we pick?"

"We must pick Lena," Birgit declared. "It's *her* birthday."

We pushed some chairs aside and all sat on the rose rug in a circle with me in the middle. I was excited and a little fearful too. Birgit went first.

"Well," Birgit said, "the truth about you, Lena, is that you draw beautifully but don't know it! I see the clothes you draw in your exercise book and . . . I don't know what to say except . . . you're awfully good, Lena. There, that's the truth."

Thea said I was a nice person and that she liked the way I recited poetry in class and that she thought I would always have many friends.

Dora's turn was next. Her voice was caressing. "Lena, you're my best friend, so I probably know you even better than anyone else here, and I love you like a sister, for you're kind and smart and clever. And that's the way you will attract a boy, for I must tell you, Lena, you are plain."

Thea protested, "That's not nice, Dora!"

Dora turned to Thea and said indignantly, "I didn't say she was *ugly*!" She turned back to me and searched my face, smiling. "Did I, Lena?"

"No," I said, confused by my feelings.

"I said Lena is plain," Dora explained to the others.

"That only means she's not pretty, and it's kinder that *we* tell her now than let her get hurt when some boy tells her!"

I felt tears sting my eyes, but I didn't want to show any of them how hard Dora's words had hit me, so I smiled as if I were grateful for the information.

"Lena has a nice figure and knows how to dress," Dora continued. "She always has. Even her dolls look better than mine!" Dora took my hand in hers. "Plain you are, Lena"—and here Dora rolled her beautiful brown eyes up at the ceiling—"but God in Heaven!— not unsightly. Not like Sala!"

"Sala wears boy boots!" Birgit cried, starting her giggling again.

Greta's turn was next, but I hardly heard what she said: "Lena, you're plain but that doesn't mean you'll *always* be plain. You'll probably become pretty later. Some girls do. And besides, some boys don't like girls who are too pretty."

I don't remember what else Greta said, because I wanted to cry but wasn't sure why. After all, I already knew I was plain, and really no girl had said anything terrible to me, yet I felt suddenly sad.

The clock in the hall struck five. Thea jumped up. "I've got to go. I promised my mother I'd be home." The other girls, realizing the time now, stood up too, and we began our *danke*s and our *auf Wiedersehen*s with cheek kisses and hugs.

When they were gone and I could no longer hear their voices down in the street, I walked into the dining room and looked at myself closely in the long

King Louis mirror. But my face seemed to merge with that of Sala's, and I turned away.

I was clearing the table when Mother came in. The room was a mess, but without commenting on it, she quietly went about picking up wrapping paper and stacking dirty plates on a tray. When we finished, she asked, "Did you have a good time?" and I told her I had. I showed her my gifts, and in that attentive way of hers, she looked carefully at each one. "You have nice friends," she said, and at these words I began to sob.

"Lena," Mother cried, "what on earth is the matter?" I couldn't tell her, for I couldn't talk. I cried and cried and at last, when I could talk, the words that came out surprised me.

"Sala," I sobbed, "it's Sala! I was mean to her!"

"How could you have been mean to her?" Mother asked. "She wasn't even here!"

"You don't understand!" I wailed. "I didn't *invite* her!"

Mother gripped my shoulders and turned me around to face her. "Why not?"

Then I told her how silly Sala was, how badly she dressed, how homely I thought she was. I told Mother how I was afraid the other girls, especially Dora, might not have liked it if Sala had been invited too. "I had to make a choice," I explained.

"It's a wicked choice," Mother replied, "because it's a choice made from fear. You can have old friends *and* new friends. You can be Dora's friend *and* Sala's too. There are no choices to make! It's how you can be

47

German *and* live in Poland. How you can be both a German *and* a Jew. You don't choose between them, do you? It's the same with friends. Don't sacrifice one to gain the other." She paused, then added, "It's a hurtful thing you've done."

"I know," I sniffled.

Mother nuzzled her warm, soft face next to my wet one. "In all decisions, Lena, listen to your heart."

We cleaned up the good room together. As I worked, I thought over what I'd do. Tomorrow at school I would talk to Sala. I would ask her to forgive me.

SIX

The next day I wanted to talk to Sala at second breakfast, but she never came to school. I didn't want the
day to end without making my apology, so after class
I asked Herr Hirschberg for her address. Students were
required to go straight home after school. If seen on
the street without a good excuse, a student risked being reported to the school by a grown-up, so I had to
lie. "I'd like to bring Sala our homework," I told Herr
Hirschberg. "I know she lives in the old town, but I
don't know exactly where." Without saying a word,
he wrote down her address.

After school I usually walked home with Dora, but
that afternoon I told her I had an errand and went in
the opposite direction. I hurried through the streets,

keeping my head slightly turned down. This way of walking was my own clever tactic. When Mother had bought the store, she had instructed me to curtsy politely to our customers when passing them on the street. But I found this so difficult that for a long time it caused me worry. So many people bought from us over the years, how could I remember who was a customer? At first I would examine every passing face. But this method proved unsuccessful. Then, when I was ten, I finally hit on it. I had only to note the person's *shoes*! As I knew our inventory well, a quick shoe-ward glance confirmed whether the passerby had ever been a customer. If yes, I curtsied.

As I went along in this eyes-down way, horses clip-clopped in the streets, pulling carriages and wagons. Every so often some estate owner's automobile rolled by, making the pedestrians stare and little children shout, "Auto! Auto!"

I went down Vovinsky Street, passing Wieski's Shoe Emporium. Our competitor, Pan Wieski, had copied Mother's idea. His window displayed ladies' shoes stuck atop crates. But his shoes were unstylish, and he had crowded too many together.

I passed our three-story synagogue with its domed roof and large tree-shaded courtyard. Three streets later I came out at the edge of the old town.

I looked at the address on the paper: 23 Timinska Street. I had no idea where that was. The narrow streets here were hundreds of years old and twisted as tangled rope. I walked down a crooked lane and ran into a flock of old women returning from the forest, their backs bent horizontally from their huge bundles of moss-covered wood. Then I turned into an alley where all about me children played—not with toys, but with stones and sticks and tin cans. They yelled back and forth to each other in Yiddish, and so in this language of which I knew little, I asked a boy of about eight where Timinska Street was.

"*Gayn hoyf,*" he chirped, pointing straight ahead. "Go to the courtyard."

I went on and in a moment came to a small courtyard with broken-down apartments on three sides. I looked around. It was obviously washday. From the lower windows stretched an assortment of shabby clothes squeezed sleeve-to-collar on makeshift clotheslines. And above, all the decaying balconies were draped with dingy, patched sheets that fluttered in the breeze. The effect was like some sort of flag day in a piteous country.

I looked at the address again, then up at the metal sign high on the apartment's brick wall: "Timinska Street." The lower apartments had the numbers 1 through 15. Figuring Sala's was upstairs, I climbed the rusted iron staircase. When I came to number 23, I knocked on the door, but there was such a wailing inside, my knocking was not heard. I knocked again and again, and at last the door was opened. Sala stood before me.

"Lena! What are you doing here!" she gasped.

"I came to bring your homework," I answered, feeling shy.

"Come in." She opened the door wider. "Please."

I walked in and found myself immediately in a tiny kitchen.

"Sit down," she ordered, heading down a hallway from where the wailing came. "I'll be right back."

I sat down at a small, rough table and looked around. Everything I saw was old. Their stove was a wood-burning one, and at the sink, instead of faucets, stood a pump. All about, things looked faded, as if over too many years their very appearance had been scrubbed away. I glanced down the shadowy hallway where Sala had gone. A blackened kerosene lamp tilted in a metal holder on the wall, and covering the floor lay two gray rugs, so small and tattered, they looked more like floor-washing rags.

Suddenly the wailing stopped and Sala stood in the doorway, her hair unevenly parted. "You brought my homework?" she asked.

"Yes," I answered, handing her the papers. "Are you sick?"

Sala laughed her inappropriate laugh. "Not me! It's my mother who's sick. That's why I stayed home, to take care of my brothers."

"Sala."

A woman's voice called weakly from a back room. Sala disappeared again and in a moment was back in the doorway, beckoning me to follow her. "My mother wants to meet you."

I followed Sala down the hall. The back room was almost as dark as the hall, for its window looked out onto the next sooty apartment. The room was unfurnished except for two iron beds: one in which Sala's mother lay, and the other in which twin babies about a year old sat gurgling. Her mother was young and her pale face pretty, but her hair was the color of dirty snow, like an old person's.

"Mameleh," Sala said, "this is Lena."

Sala's mother smiled and extended her thin hand. "It's nice to meet you," she said in Yiddish, then turning her face to Sala said, "Bring me some tea and give some to your friend too . . . and give her bread."

As I followed Sala back into the kitchen, I told her primly, "Thank you, but I'm really not hungry." The truth was I had as much desire to take food in this hovel as dine at a rat catcher's picnic. But Sala ignored my words and told me to sit at the table. She pumped water into the kettle, lit some kindling, and put the kettle on the stove.

While she prepared the tea, neither she nor I said a word. She poured tea into three glasses and took one to her mother. When she returned, she stirred into our glasses a spoonful of jam, Russian style. From a curtained cupboard beneath the sink she pulled out two plates, chipped but clean, and placed on each a slice of bread she cut from a loaf that sat on a splintery shelf.

Sala put the food on the table, then sat opposite me. "Eat," she said.

I did, and though there was no butter for the bread, I found it surprisingly delicious, especially when dunked ever so slightly into the tea, as Sala told me to do. If I hadn't felt their poverty so much, I would have accepted her offer of a second slice.

The shouts of the children in the alley were the

only sounds that broke our awkward silence. As we ate, I suddenly thought how unnecessary it might be to apologize to Sala. After all, Sala might not even have known that I'd had a party! But as I drank the tea, I realized that I had to apologize for *me*, so I said quickly, "I'm very sorry I didn't invite you to my party. It wasn't nice to have left you out."

Sala's face reddened at my words. For a moment she said nothing. Then she said softly, "It's all right. I didn't want to go."

"You didn't want to go to my party?" I asked in surprise.

"No."

"Why not?"

"Because I don't have a party dress . . . and because . . ."

"Because what?"

"Because you're not my friend."

The bluntness of her reply threw me off guard. I considered it while I sat chewing. It sounded logical.

"I *could* be your friend," I said. "I mean it's not that I don't like you or anything. And we have things in common, like our school and nasty old Hirschberg and our choir and we're both Jewish too."

Sala did not reply to any of this. One of the babies started to howl in the back room, and she left to tend it. When she returned, she sat down with the toddler on her lap. She didn't say a word. I wondered whether she wanted me to go.

"Perhaps, Sala, on Sunday, you could come to our house? My mother always has gefilte fish left over from Shabbos, and we could walk together to City Park. Would you like that?" Then, so she wouldn't think I was talking charity, I added, "I'd like it."

Slowly a smile broke across Sala's face, and without warning she hummed a Schubert melody.

It was her way of saying yes, and it was the way our friendship began.

SEVEN

At first our friendship had a big element of business in it. I believed that if I could get Sala to dress nicer, our classmates would stop making fun of her. To this end I cooked up several money-making plans.

One Sunday morning, without telling Sala what was in my mind, I made her come into the synagogue with me, for I wanted to speak to Goat Welmer. Goat Welmer was our *Vorsteher*—our synagogue manager. I don't know if I had ever heard his real name, for children and grown-ups alike called him "Goat" because of his short, round body, shaggy, pointed beard, and gruff manner. "Never butt heads with the Goat!" went the congregant wisdom. Forget your charity payments, and he'd be at your door fast as a Prussian tax collector. Arrive late to service, and you'd be scolded before God Himself. But Goat's gruff manner was a bluff, for he was one of the kindest people I knew.

I rushed up the long aisle of our synagogue, with Sala, nervous and giggly, running behind me. As we hurried along in the empty sanctuary, its grand elegance wrapped about us. The great hall soared upward, capped by a vaulted dome in gold, red, and blue tiles from which hung brass chandeliers the size of rowboats. Tall, arched windows flooded the interior with light that sparkled on these chandeliers and danced off the mosaic tile floor. Beneath the windows the high gallery in which the women and girls sat was enclosed by ironwork that curled into a thousand leaves and flowers.

Sala and I raced up the aisle, the long pews on either side of us stretching away like crop furrows. When we arrived at the bimah, the platform from where our Torah is read, we paused. Around the bimah four twisted marble columns supported an immense marble capital engraved with the German words *Alles was Odem hat, lobt den Herrn! Halleluja!* Let every thing that hath breath praise the Lord. Hallelujah.

"I've never been this close to the bimah!" exclaimed Sala. She stretched out her hand to feel the coldness of the marble column.

"HAVE YOU NO REVERENCE FOR THE HOUSE OF GOD!"

We turned to see Goat Welmer standing behind us, his eyes blazing.

"What are you doing in synagogue at this worldly

time?!" he shouted. "Click-clacking your girlie shoes to wake the dead! Hurrying about and fingering things like shoppers! Fingering *holy* things! Hurrying in a *holy* place!" Goat Welmer fixed his angry brown eyes first on my face, then on Sala's, before he again roared, "HAVE YOU NO REVERENCE FOR THE HOUSE OF GOD!"

From the corner of my eye I could see Sala's face turn pale and hear her breathing quicken.

"Yes, Herr Welmer," I answered. "We have reverence; that's why we're here! My friend Sala hates to see waste. Especially in the House of God! It's wicked!"

He looked at me in amazement. Before he could speak, I said, "Herr Welmer, we came to ask you a question. May Sala collect the globs of wax that drip from the Shabbos candles?"

Sala turned to me, stupefied, and Goat stared at me as if I'd lost my wits. "Oh, Sala would be very quiet and neat about it," I told him.

Goat Welmer looked long at Sala, and the anger drained from his face as he began to understand my purpose. Without saying a word, he walked toward the altar and stopped at the table upon which stood two brass candlesticks, each about three feet tall. The candlesticks were encrusted with mounds of melted wax that had dripped during the Shabbos services. We three stood around this table, and he said to Sala, "I suppose it would save me a deal of cleaning time if you were to take away the wax late on a Sunday morning."

"Thank you, Herr Welmer," Sala mumbled, not knowing what in the world was going on.

"Thank you, Herr Welmer," I said, wanting now to go.

But Goat, attempting to resume his grumpiness, wagged his finger at Sala and warned, "Mind you, don't make a mess! No dropping wax on the floor. God's house is not where pious Jews should slip and break their fanny bones!"

"No, Herr Welmer," I said.

"No, Herr Welmer," Sala copied.

We turned and walked very slowly and very quietly back down the aisle until we came out of the synagogue into the courtyard.

As soon as we got outside, Sala burst out laughing. She leaned against the brick wall of the courtyard and howled, "Fanny bones!" She laughed so hard she began to hiccup, and her drunken sound started me laughing too. We laughed like witches. As soon as one of us caught her breath, the other whispered, "Fanny bones!" and we'd start shrieking all over again, wiping our eyes and nearly wetting our pants. We tried the words out in the most unlikely voices.

"FANNY BONES!" I shouted angrily, as Herr Hirschberg might call up the name of a girl to be slapped.

"Faaaanny Boooones," Sala chanted in the solemn, holy way of Rabbi Fried.

"Do you have first-quality fanny bones?" I asked in the nasal voice of our most stuck-up lady customer. "Show me the largest size!" We laughed ourselves

silly at our parodies, doubled over as if with stom-
achaches. Then, just when I thought we were all
laughed out, Sala exclaimed, "Oy! What will
Mameleh and I do with wax! Spread it on toast?" At
this image we both laughed afresh, screaming and
snorting wildly, clutching each other for support in
our senseless mirth. But after several minutes we did
stop, for our sides began to hurt.

Then I explained my idea. "I'll give you shoe boxes
to pack the wax in. At the end of each month you sell
the wax to Ragman Flinker. He'll give you five zlotys
for every pound of it—if it's clean."

"Five zlotys?" Sala asked dreamily.

"Yes, and look." I picked up some of the chestnuts
that had fallen in the courtyard. "You could sell these
to him too. We ate them in wartime, though they're
not the nice eating kind. Flinker sells them to a place
in Koeva where they use them to make glue. He'll
give you four zlotys a pound."

And I had other ideas for Sala. I showed her how to
pick dry grass, chop it, and sew it into heart-shaped
pincushions, which we began to sell in our store. On
Sundays after her wax collecting Sala and I gathered
poziomki, the small wild strawberries that grow in
the forest. We packed the *poziomki* in baby-shoe
boxes. Then we stood at the side of the road waiting
with our little harvest for customers. However, this
enterprise was cut short when Mother received an unsigned letter expressing indignation that Jewish children should "take away agricultural business from
Poles."

"Get your teeth into a profit," the letter said, "and the Jew rips it out of your mouth."

Though we had to give up strawberries, Sala made a nice twenty zlotys a month from wax, chestnuts, and pincushions. Yet my plans were not successful, as Sala spent not one zloty on improving her appearance. She gave all her earnings to her mother for food.

I began to realize that even if Sala had dressed like the other girls, she was so different from them, she would never fit in. I remained her only friend. In spring, kind-hearted Thea would join us in our walks to City Park, but more often Sala and I went alone. We found a special, private place in the park, a soft grassy knoll in the shade of an ash tree. This spot we called our Daisy Dell, and here we returned every Sunday to make necklaces from what we called "doll daisies," the tiny white flowers that sprout in the grass. I loved these Sundays, for I could tell my most secret thoughts to Sala better than to anyone I knew. She never laughed her wild laugh at them. I told Sala how much I still missed Ta Ta and often dreamed of him at night. I confessed that deep down inside I feared I was ugly. I told her how much I adored the poetry of Goethe. I confided how I thought I could be a really good seamstress one day. One weekend when Günther came back to visit, I was so excited, I talked to Sala about him for days afterward. I bragged shamelessly about his new part-time job as a journalist for the *Berliner Tageblatt*. "And he's barely twenty!" I boasted.

I told Sala so many things, but she told me nothing.

I was full of curiosity about her too. I wanted to know why, if her mother was a Polish Jew, Sala went to our German school. I wanted to know where her father was. And above all, I wanted to know why they were so poor.

If I asked her a question, though, she'd ignore it, change the subject, or mumble, "I don't know."

But I had a trick to get answers. I'd thread a personal question into the cloth of general discussion: "Don't you think, Sala, that getting letters is one of the nicest things? Thea told me she gets letters every month from her pen friends—though I bet you get a lot from your father, don't you?" or "Tante Ilse says sewing is a good job. She makes nice money at it. Do you think your mother would want to try it?"

After weeks of this sneaky talk, I learned only a little. I learned that Sala's father was a German Jew from Ledniezno, but after they married, her parents moved to her mother's hometown, Grajewo. For a while they lived well, but just before her brothers were born, Sala's father died of typhus. Her mother brought the family back here because she thought Sala's grandfather would help them. Besides, she wanted Sala to go to a German school, as there was much anti-Semitism in the Polish schools. But after arriving here, the old grandfather died and Sala's mother was forced to pay his debts! Now she was ill, and they lived on their small savings.

"But what will happen when your savings are gone?" I asked, though it was none of my business. "There are few jobs for Jews. How will you live?"

"I don't know," Sala answered softly.

These were the true things Sala told me. But she did another kind of telling—storytelling—for she lived as well in an imaginary world where life was happier and very beautiful. Much of her true talk was embroidered with pretty lies—in the same way that peasants sew colorful stitches onto their work shirts just to make them cheerier.

At first I got annoyed when she told me she once rode in a glass coach, understood the talk of cats, or was descended from a Babylonian princess. But as I spent more time with Sala, I came to actually welcome her lies, for they turned my Sunday afternoons into entertainment.

Sala even got me pretending too. She and I liked to pretend we were stage actresses. We would jump up on the oak stump and, in quavering voices, recite to each other with much waving of arms and rolling of eyes. My favorite verses were from Goethe's *Trilogy of Passion*. It was all about a man grieving for his lost love yet reminding himself that despite his own sorrow, the world remained beautiful—even holy. " 'Are not even the rocks crowned with sacred shadows?' " I would intone.

Sala too had a favorite poem she loved to quote with mournful melodrama:

> *"When the world lies heavy upon my soul,*
> *I shall not hear the bells that toll.*
> *For upon a bower I'll lay me down*
> *And flee forever the indifferent town. . . ."*

Now, at first I didn't know Sala's dream; but as she had a way of pondering things aloud, a few months after our friendship began, I learned it.

We were in the Daisy Dell stringing necklaces from the doll daisies. It was a warm summer Sunday, cloudless and calm. Sala, who had been quiet for a while as if listening to something, suddenly said, "I wonder what a forest sounds like on a piano."

I laughed. "You can't play a forest on a piano!"

"I could play a forest," she insisted, "and though I've never seen one, I could play an ocean too . . . and all the creatures in it." She paused to consider her boast for a moment, then added matter-of-factly, "I could play the world."

I didn't respond to this, for it sounded silly—like more storytelling. But then, unbidden, Sala spun her most improbable tale. She told me that at the age of six she had begun taking piano lessons from her uncle Vladimir, who had once played at the court of Czar Nicholas II. Sala claimed she had learned to play music by Schubert, Brahms, and Beethoven. She told me how she longed to study at the Poznań Conservatory of Music. She said it was a terrible pity to her that now in Ledniezno she couldn't practice. "I have no piano and will never, ever have a piano," she sighed.

Fairy Tale Number 427, I thought, yet I let her go on. And go on she did. It was as if once Sala had told her story, she could not stop telling it. From that day on we were never together without her mentioning her uncle or Beethoven or how she might play a particular piece of music. One Sunday as we passed the cathedral on the way to the park, we saw on the sidewalk the old organ grinder churning out a waltz. This patchwork Gypsy had beside him an upturned derby to catch the coins from worshipers as they filed out of mass. We listened to the music for some moments; then Sala said, more to herself than to me, " *'Der Frühling'*! It's the loveliest of waltzes! But it mustn't go that fast. Uncle Vladimir told me when you play it, you must think of a lady on a swing slowly pushed by her lover."

Sala's voice had such a yearning in it that right then I too wished she had a piano to play, and a thought came into my mind. I turned her around to face me and solemnly asked, "Sala, can you *really* play the piano?"

She did not say yes but nodded.

"Well then," I said, my voice rising with excitement, "would you like a piano to practice on every day—even if it wasn't your own?"

"I don't need my very own," she answered vaguely.

"Then come on!" I grabbed Sala's hand, pulling her along as I went quickly up the street.

"Where are we going?"

"I've got an idea; just come on!"

We rushed through the streets, my idea growing larger as we went, blossoming like a great beautiful flower. We hurried up Bierkaut Road, then went down Dienko Street, passing one grand house after another until we came to the grandest house of all. We looked up at the great three-story brick mansion. A long flight of marble stairs swept upward to the elegantly carved front door with its eagle-head brass knocker.

I turned to Sala. "Dora's house."

"I don't understand," Sala said.

"In their good room," I explained, "the Gerhardts have the very most beautiful piano. A grand piano, black and shiny as patent leather. I'm going to ask Frau Gerhardt whether you can come after school and practice on it!" I watched Sala's face to witness there the joyous response to my clever idea. But her eyes grew wide with fear, and she protested madly.

"Oh no, Lena, I can't! I can't! Not in Dora's house!"

"Why not?"

"She doesn't like me!"

"Grow up, Sala! Whether Dora likes you or not has nothing to do with it. I'll ask her *mother*, not her. I'll ask her as Dora's friend. Dora and I, you know, have been best friends for ages!"

"But they're . . . they're . . ." Sala stammered.

"They're what?" I demanded.

"Evangelical!"

"So? What's that got to do with pickle prices in Pinsk? Most Germans are!"

"Yes, but . . ." Sala mumbled nervously.

"But nothing! You've been moaning about how you would love a piano to play, and this is the only piano I know. I'm being very nice to use my friendship with Dora to help *you*! So tuck in your blouse and come on!"

Sala sighed and carelessly shoved in her blouse. Then, like a prisoner walking to her execution, she followed me up the long stairs.

EIGHT

Hedwig, the maid, opened the door. She smiled at me but completely ignored Sala as she led us into the lofty hallway. When she left to get Dora, Sala stared wide-eyed at everything as if she were in a museum. She touched everything too. She felt the lace of the runner on the mahogany table. She held her palms against the cold brass of the Indian vase, and she floated her fingertips slowly along the velvet-flocked wallpaper as if reading Braille.

"Lena, I'm so glad you're here! Mother's bought ice cream from Schenken's and we're having it for coffee-klatsch!" Dora sailed into the hall to greet me and we hugged. She was wearing a new blue dress, and around her neck was looped a scarf with Egyptian hieroglyphics—the latest fad. Dora's hair was done in a charming array of small curls. Seeing my surprise at her new look, she twirled, her laughs ringing like chimes down the long hall. At first Dora didn't even see Sala, for she had floated right past her. But suddenly she stopped and exclaimed, "Sala! Imagine seeing you here!"

Sala blushed, pulling nervously at her droopy hair.

"We want to talk to your mother," I told Dora. "We want to ask her whether Sala could come after school and practice on your piano." From the expression on Dora's face I could tell she thought this was a bad idea, but I took her arm affectionately and whispered, "Please, Dora, let me speak to your mother."

Dora led us into the good room, and soon, in a whiff of lovely perfume, Frau Gerhardt entered. Sala and I curtsied, and I explained the purpose of our visit. All the while I was speaking, Frau Gerhardt stared at Sala, and when I finished, she composed her face, turned it back to me, and spoke kindly. "Lena, dear, you're a very sweet girl to worry so much about your little classmate, but I must tell you that our good room is not a piano studio, and it would be highly inconvenient if it were to be used in this way. I'm sorry it won't work out, but we have nice ice cream for you."

I glanced at Sala and thought I saw relief rather than disappointment. However, I was disappointed, and so, unwisely, I argued with Frau Gerhardt.

"But Sala is almost a concert pianist!" I said recklessly. "Her uncle played for a czar of Russia! She's learned everything from him, and she is so very good that she could be a wonderful teacher for Dora!"

Frau Gerhardt said nothing to this, but Dora laughed, winking at me from her armchair, as if the two of us were putting some colossal lie over on her mother. I thought then that the plan was lost, but Frau Gerhardt gave Dora a sharp look of warning, turned back to me, and said, "I will consider this lesson idea. Let her play and then I shall decide." I looked triumphantly at Sala, but she did not move toward the piano.

"Play the piano," I whispered. "Go on!"

Slowly Sala stood up and walked over to the beautiful instrument. She stroked the white bust of some composer atop it, then sat down on the piano bench. For a long while she stared down at the keys.

I looked at the sky out the window. "God," I prayed, "please make her get on with it!"

My prayers were useless, and as Sala continued to stare dumbly at the keyboard, a horrible thought took hold. What if Sala's piano playing was just another lie? My mind raced back to the look of fear in her eyes when I had suggested coming here. If she really could play, I reasoned—now too late—she would have been ecstatic at my idea, not scared! How could I have believed that in her poor life, Sala could have learned to play Beethoven! And worse, how could I have been so stupid as to let Sala humiliate me in front of my best friend!

In the long silence I was in agony. I felt at any moment I'd burst into tears. I glanced over at Sala. She was still sitting motionless.

"Go on, Sala," I pleaded.

But she did nothing until at last she said, "I can't play."

Dora made a mock gasping sound, and I felt tears sting my eyes. I went over to Sala and urged her frantically. "Yes you can! You *said* you can play, so you will."

"No, I can't. I need a cushion. I can't play without another cushion under me."

Dora stifled a laugh.

"Give the girl a cushion," Frau Gerhardt impatiently commanded her daughter, pointing to a Chinese one on the settee.

Sala took the embroidered cushion from Dora and, in her infuriatingly slow way, tucked it under her, then bounced her bottom on it several times to flatten it down. But when she had finished, she just continued to sit. Her hands were not even poised over the keys but folded on her lap. As if sitting for a portrait! I dared not look at Frau Gerhardt, for I knew in the next moment she would call the whole thing a thoughtless prank. She'd report the incident to my mother and Herr Hirschberg too. But in the next moment something else happened—Sala's hands rose from her lap and hovered over the keys.

At first she touched the keys very gently, as if she were afraid of breaking them. The sound she made was soft, almost inaudible, like the sound of your own heart. But then she put other sounds with it, and the piano came alive, speaking in a voice. Sala's scuffed shoes worked the pedals with a dancer's skill, and on either side of the long keyboard her arms were stretched wide as a saint's. Sala's fingers flew over the keys, coaxing and caressing them until the piano spoke in several voices at once, as if it were singing a great choral ballad. Then I understood it—Sala was playing the forest! She was playing pine trees soaring into the sky, damp leafy earth, fast nervous squirrels, hopeful songs of birds.

Then she played the ocean! The rolling deep of it and its cold, dark secrets. She played waves crashing, shipwrecks, unseen writhing creatures. She played the ominous sound of a storm approaching, the rhythmic breath of tides. It was music she played, yet it was something beyond music too. I glanced at Dora's mother to see if Sala's performance instilled in her the wonder it did in me. But her face was turned from the piano, her eyes fixed at some point over the mantel. Yet I knew then that whatever Dora's mother might decide, Sala had told the truth. For that afternoon in the Gerhardts' good room, Sala played the world.

NINE

1925–1928

My plan for Sala to practice on the Gerhardts' piano succeeded brilliantly. Frau Gerhardt arranged for Sala to give Dora piano lessons twice a week at five zlotys a lesson. What's more, she permitted Sala to stay up to an hour afterward to practice.

A few months after Sala started giving lessons, she dropped out of our class. Her mother could no longer afford the Higher German Daughters' School and was forced to send her to the Polish public school. But soon she dropped out of that school as well. She stayed home to help her mother and was so busy, she almost never had time to see me. And so as the year wore on, I concerned myself less with Sala and more with myself.

I combed my hair for hours in front of the King Louis mirror, sometimes pasting the curls on my cheeks like an actress and other times pinning my hair to the top of my head like a ballerina. I wore my skirts backward—buttons all down the front; wore my school cap at a jaunty angle; tied my black hair ribbon around my neck. It seemed I was always trying to look like someone else, and perhaps be someone else too, though I did not know who.

My mother bought me an old sewing machine, and by the time I was fourteen, I was making my own clothes. I started with store-bought patterns, then made my own patterns from designs I saw in magazines, and later—designs I saw in my mind. My dressmaking skill made me someone special among my friends. Within the year I was earning good pocket money by sewing up simple patterns for girlfriends.

At that time too I began to go out much more. I'd go to Schenken's café with Dora, Birgit, Greta, and Thea. We would order coffee with cream and pretend we were eighteen. Sometimes Greta would try to persuade one of us to send a note via the waiter to some young soldier at another table. None of us ever dared do this, yet just the suggestion of performing such a flirtation kept us in excited whispers. Just as much fun was going with Greta to the newly opened cinema. Films were at first shown only on Saturdays, but luckily there was a late show after Shabbos ended at sunset. Arms linked, Greta and I would stroll there in the evening and for hours eat apples and stare up at Douglas Fairbanks.

At fifteen I opened to the world, becoming more and more restless. It seemed then I wanted to reach out and touch all the things I had read about in books. I yearned for beauty and romance. I dreamed of waltzing with handsome boys in Vienna, sipping coffee in the cafés of Paris, dancing in a ballet.

And so in my own dreamy, fanciful time, it was a blow when Mother received her first death threat.

Like the other hateful letters sent to our store, it was unsigned. This writer said we were unpatriotic, for we had not displayed a flag on our store for Polish Independence Day and other state holidays. If this "treasonous omission" were to happen again, the letter warned, we would pay a price in blood!

Mother did not open the letter until we got home, and when she read it, her face was on fire. I was reading it too, over her shoulder—and just as I'd finished, she tore the letter into dozens of little scraps and threw them into the stove. Then, completely unlike her, she broke down and cried. Each sob was a knife cutting through the hopeful world in my mind.

"Mother," I pleaded, holding her hand in my own, "nothing bad will happen. I can make a flag. I will sew a big one, and we'll hang it from the store window this year so that this 'patriot' won't have a thing to say against us!"

Mother wiped her eyes and asked fiercely, "We always have a flag flying from our home on Independence Day. Why do we need one on the store too?"

"It's not a matter of *need*, it's a matter of *appearance*. I'll buy the cloth tomorrow."

She stroked my cheek ever so gently with the back of her hand. "You're a smart girl."

It was when she said this that the fearful thought came into my mind and I asked, "Mother, do you think it was a good idea to tear up the letter? I mean maybe we should have kept it as evidence."

She did not reply, and at once I regretted my words. Jewish evidence was almost never taken seriously in a Polish court of law.

At last Mother said in a forced cheerful voice, "Lena, let's not talk of this anymore. There's nothing we can do about it now, and really, it's not worth our breath! We know that all this ugliness will go away. I have hope it will be soon."

I said no more but could not embrace her hope. It seemed to me that Mother was too trusting. After the war Mother had trusted in the Versailles Treaty. Now Mother trusted in Josef Pilsudski, who last May had seized control of the government. "Pilsudski will modernize Poland," she had explained to me. "He will rid Poland of anti-Semitism." Yet months had passed and the hatred against us had not lessened. Our city newspaper, *Lech*, exhorted the citizens not to buy from any business owned by a Jew. *"SWOJ DO SWEGO!"* the headlines urged: "STICK TO YOUR OWN KIND!" The prejudice against us was encouraged by many in the middle and upper classes. They despised the great masses of poor, highly religious Jews who dressed in black medieval clothes and spoke Yiddish, but even more, they resented the assimilated, middle-class Jews who owned businesses. In their minds a Jewish business by its very existence was a threat to the success of a Christian one.

It was only due to Mother's cleverness that we survived as well as we did. She was indulgent toward our customers. She often told me, "Don't open a shop unless you know how to smile." Even more important, Mother had style. After all, where else could a chic lady such as Frau Gerhardt buy lizard-skin pumps from Milan or kid dancing slippers from Paris? Where could she get fashion advice and attentive service? Not at Wieski's Emporium! From Danzig to Poznań, not anywhere but at our store. Katz Fine Shoes. And Frau Gerhardt, though a German, was so admired for her beauty and taste that the local Polish women bought from us merely because they knew *she* bought from us.

Our survival was also due to the good relations we had with some of the peasants. They were poor, most of them, and went barefoot. Besides their winter boots, they owned one other pair of special "town shoes," which they carried and put on only upon entering the town. For them, buying shoes was a major event, something they did only once every several years.

With these people who had little cash, we bartered. They would bring us apples, or vegetables, or sometimes down pillows and quilts. We would give them shoes. They could, of course, have bought much cheaper shoes from the stalls in the marketplace. But many of the peasants, despite their rough ways, knew and wanted quality. They wanted sturdy, long-lasting, heavy leather shoes. Some of these customers were kind to us. On Christmas or at Easter we would sometimes find on our front steps a small gift: a knitted cap, a cheese, an embroidered handkerchief. Our culture and that of the Polish peasants were vastly different, yet in this precarious country our livelihoods wove together like threads on a rickety loom.

Despite these good customers, though, we saw the truth. We were Germans and we were Jews living in a country that did not want either.

How happy I was then when, only a month after the letter came, Mother announced we would visit Berlin. "We're going to see Günther!" I crowed. "We're going to see Tante Ilse!"

"Yes, we are," Mother said, "but that's not all. I've been thinking perhaps it is time we leave Poland. Perhaps it is time to move to Germany. We're going to look at apartments in Berlin."

Apartments in Berlin! My joy knew no bounds. The idea of living not only in our Fatherland but in the grand city of Berlin was more thrilling news than I could stand. I packed at once, singing my German school songs all the while.

TEN

Berlin, Germany
October 15, 1927

Slip into the time-annihilating tea dress with its caressing draperies of soft crepe de Chine and lace. For remember, it is in the twilight hour when afternoon fades that Woman forgets the march of centuries and becomes the incarnation of that eternal feminine that knows no era . . . but is of all time.

I reread the pretty hand-lettered sign inside the store window. Then I let my eyes move slowly upward to the gown that was the color of ripe apricots.

"Mother, isn't it the most exquisite dress!"

"It is," Mother agreed. "But Lena, this is only the first store, and we have a long way to go!" We were standing on the Kurfürstendamm in Berlin. The night train from Poznań had arrived at nine A.M., and since Tante Ilse and Günther were working at this time, Mother said we could have a whole day of sightseeing before meeting them in the evening.

"Wasn't it you who wanted to see," Mother said, counting on her fingers, "the Brandenburg Gate, the Great Synagogue, Charlottenburg Palace, the Reichstag, Bellevue Palace, the Tiergarten, Unter den Linden Palace, the Opera House, and the botanical garden!"

"Yes, but I didn't know the Berlin stores would be this grand!" And so, because she wanted very much to please me that day, we walked slowly along the immense shopping boulevard, gazing into one opulent store after another. My eyes drank in the riches: wine velvet cloche hats, blue satin party pajamas, red ostrich-feather fans, black stockings dotted with rhinestones along the seams, and silk handbags in the shape of roses with matching rose-patterned scarves!

Just as wonderful were the shoe stores. Mother was as fascinated by them as I was. We stared into the windows, marveling at shoes, some costing one billion marks. "Look at those Perugia pumps!" she gasped. "Covered entirely in lace! Look at the dancing slippers studded with garnets!"

"And look!" I cried. "Look at the Ferragamo shoes with spiral brass heels!"

Every new thing I saw made me joyful, and so, to keep each one forever—without buying it—I drew whatever I most loved in my sketchbook. Until well past noon Mother and I strolled spellbound through the sumptuous streets, and I recorded every entrancing thing. For not only did the store windows of Berlin hold for me a magical world of beauty, but the wide streets themselves made a magnificent promenade. Making our way down the Kurfürstendamm, Mother and I were just a tiny part of a great movement. The revolving glass doors of the department stores and the decoratively etched entrances of the cafés spilled out perfumed ladies in furs and gentlemen sporting monocles. The profusion of flowers sold by the street vendors, the stately grace of autumn chestnut trees, and the important clack of smart shoes on the sidewalk made me giddy. And through it all wound the wonderfully familiar cultured sounds of German, *our* language. We are Germans among Germans, I mused gaily.

When at last our feet grew tired, we found ourselves in front of an enormous café. Jazz music wailed out the door, and Mother surprised me by saying, "Here's where we'll have lunch." Inside, I could barely eat, for I was too busy sneaking glances at the chic women. Their hair bobbed and oiled, their eyes rimmed with black makeup, their cheeks and earlobes rouged, their dresses short and swingy—these women enchanted me; they waved long cigarette holders like magic wands and sat not only on chairs but on the tables too, their thin legs pointing down dangerously as crossed swords.

I could tell by Mother's expression that she greatly disapproved of what she had often called "girls with male hairdressing" and regretted coming in. But I leaned across the table and whispered knowingly, "Flappers."

Mother did not reply. She merely ate faster and over the loud music urged me not to dawdle. She paid the bill promptly, and I followed her out the door.

We then had about three hours before we were due at Tante Ilse's, so we decided to walk to the Reichstag—the Parliament building—in the Platz der Republik. But before we even reached the corner, we heard angry yelling.

Two men in brown shirts with the National Socialist party emblem, the swastika, on their sleeves, were standing in front of a small group of pedestrians and yelling their party philosophy. As we walked past, the younger of the uniformed men thrust a flyer into my hand.

BACK-STABBING CRIMINALS HAVE PLOTTED TREASON AND STILL ARE PLOTTING TREASON! THEY STEAL OUR MONEY AND BRING RUIN AND POVERTY TO YOU HARDWORKING GERMANS! WITH THEIR FILTHY, PRIMITIVE, GREEDY MORALITY, THEY POISON OUR NATION, OUR CULTURE, AND OUR BLOOD!

"Mother, look at this!" I said, holding the flyer in front of her. But she wouldn't even look at the flyer. Before I could finish reading it, and not caring who might see, she grabbed the flyer from my hand and threw it into the gutter. "That is where that belongs!" she said, and the tone in her voice meant, "We will not even speak of it." So without a word I walked beside her as we crossed the square to the enormous German Parliament building. Standing in front of this famous place, I felt as if we'd come on a pilgrimage to a sacred site. The grand building embodied for me everything that was beautiful and great in my German culture, and the Reichstag's inscription, TO THE GERMAN PEOPLE, made me think proudly of Father and the Germany he had fought for. We walked about the Reichstag, marveling at its enormous pillars, Greek sculptures, and glass cupola.

Then Mother and I strolled along the immaculate paths of the Tiergarten, the large park across from the square. We took coffee in a small café in the park, sitting outside where we could watch rowboats on the lake.

At last, in the late afternoon we boarded the trolley. The trolley rolled quickly past the long streets of elegant mansions, and then it seemed we rode for miles through streets of decaying apartments where jobless men hung around like left baggage. It seemed too that on every streetcorner I saw beggars. Some of them wheeled their pathetic possessions in wheelbarrows or old baby carriages. Some still wore their war uniforms! At one corner, I think near the Brunnenstrasse stop, an entire family sat on the pavement, each member holding a receptacle—a cup, a cap, a can— for receiving coins.

We got off the trolley in the tidy district of Reinickendorf and walked a short distance to Tante Ilse's apartment. The small apartment building had four flights of stairs, and I was so eager to see her, I abandoned ladylike deportment and bounded up them two at a time.

"How you can hike through Berlin all day, yet have the energy to leap up stairs!" Mother exclaimed from below. "My feet are killing me!"

"Your shoes are no good!" I called down impudently as I raced to the top. "Find yourself a good shoe store!"

"Lena Katz! I can hear your sassy voice from my kitchen, and all the neighbors can too! Close your mouth and give your auntie a hug!" Tante Ilse stood scolding me at her open front door. In mock anger, my plump aunt stood with her hands firmly on her hips, reminding me of a sugar bowl.

Instead of curtsying, I hugged her hard, nearly lifting her off her feet. After kissing me, Tante Ilse embraced my mother. They held each other for a long time. Then my aunt stood back in her tiny good room to view me. "Haven't you grown tall, and look at your thick curly hair! Lena, you've become pretty!"

I smiled but was not flattered, for this was prejudiced family talk; it had nothing to do with reality.

"And where did you get that clever blouse?" Tante Ilse asked. "Did Pani Poyarska make it?"

"*I* made it," I answered proudly, for I was quite pleased about the complicated Vogue pattern I'd sewn.

"You!" Tante Ilse cried. "Your mother wrote me you could sew nicely, but I didn't know you could do such advanced work. Lena, you sew as well as I—maybe better! Come."

Grabbing my hand, she led me back to her bedroom, with Mother following behind. There, hanging on a rack next to her sewing machine, hung a lavender georgette dress with a scoop neck and three flounces at the skirt. "How do you like this?" Tante Ilse asked me. "I made it for a customer who's going to a wedding."

"It's lovely," I answered, then perhaps being a little too bold, added, "it'd be especially nice if you trimmed the flounces with violet ribbon."

"Violet ribbon?"

"Yes, it would accent the dress so well—make it more dramatic—and violet is such a romantic color."

Tante Ilse did not laugh at this but stared in silence at the dress.

"Trim is not part of the pattern, and it is really quite nice the way it is," Mother said soothingly, for perhaps she thought her sister's feelings were hurt.

"Nonsense! The girl's right!" exclaimed Tante Ilse. "And I'll make a matching cloche hat trimmed with violet ribbon too."

"Adorned with a sprig of silk violets," I said.

"Perfect!" sang Tante Ilse. "Lena, you talk like a magazine." Then going to her closet, she took from its shelf a big blue box wrapped with blue ribbon and held it out in my direction.

"For me?"

"Who else?"

Pulling off the ribbon, I drew out a large green rush-

and-cane sewing basket that stood on four brass legs.
"Oh! Thank you, Tante Ilse!"

"Open the lid," she commanded.

I did and found that the interior, lined with tufted emerald-green satin, held two dozen spools of colored thread, a package of tailor's chalk, a green cloth measuring tape, a heart-shaped ivory box for needles, a green satin pin cushion, brass scissors, and a brass thimble.

"Do you like it?" she asked.

"I love it!"

"Good!" Tante Ilse chuckled. "If you can make such fashionable clothes as that blouse and dream up dress trim, you need a real seamstress's kit, for I'm sure you'll make a very good seamstress one day."

"I always thought she had talent," Mother agreed.

"AND WHY DON'T *I* GET A SEWING BOX? WHY MUST MEN ALWAYS BE DISCRIMINATED AGAINST!"

Startled, we turned at the deep voice to see, at the bedroom door, a tall man with dark hair and wire spectacles.

"Günther!" I shrieked, then flew into my brother's open arms.

That evening our supper was a happy one. We were a family again, arguing, laughing, and remembering all together. We talked all together too, interrupting each other, speaking at the same time. I suppose if we had not been a family, it would have seemed rude. But

that night our love for each other and our joy at being together made us raucous as children.

Across the dining table I gazed in awe at Günther. It had been only a year since he had visited us in Ledniezno, yet he seemed to have become a man in that year. There was no child left in him except perhaps his boyish enthusiasm for journalism. He worked for Berlin's largest newspaper, the *Berliner Tageblatt*, and was so informed about so many things, I felt quite stupid when he spoke. He seemed to me the most knowledgeable person on Earth.

While accepting another slice of Tante Ilse's tender sauerbraten, he said to me, "So today you've been discovering Berlin."

"Yes, and I adore it. It's *so* much grander than Ledniezno."

"Can't compare castles with cabins!" He laughed. "Berlin is the most exciting city in Europe. For great literature, great theater, great music, great thought— come to Berlin!"

"We will come to Berlin," Mother said, "as soon as I can sell the store, settle affairs, and find an apartment."

"Wise move," Tante Ilse pronounced, helping herself to her own delicious roast potatoes. "I told you years ago Germans belong in Germany, but you were stubborn."

Mother, bristling slightly, replied, "I wanted to save as much as I could first, so when I come to Germany I'll have money in my pocket."

"Perhaps your decision to stay in Poland wasn't so bad at the time," Tante Ilse conceded. "You've made money. But now you must leave. Pilsudski will not be able to change the minds of anti-Semites. May their eyes run!"

"Mother," Günther said gently, "you'll be leaving Poland just in time. The Poles resent successful Jews, but in Germany we're rewarded. Germany is now a member of the League of Nations. We have a democracy in which Jews are treated as well as anyone."

"But what," I asked cautiously, "is Germany going to do about the back-stabbing criminals?"

A silence fell over the table. "Someone tell the child," cried Tante Ilse as she left the table.

"Lena," Mother explained, "*we* are called the back-stabbing criminals. Jews are accused of being criminals by some Germans who blame us for losing the war."

"But Jews fought in the war!" I cried. "Ta Ta *died* for Germany!"

"Of course there's no *truth* in their accusation," Günther explained to me. "It's just one of the Nazis' tactics."

Carrying in her poppyseed cake, Tante Ilse scowled. "Nazis! May a disease enter their gums!"

"Tante, they need educating," said Günther. And here his voice grew fervent with belief. "Many Jewish journalists and teachers travel in groups to the small towns. They arrange meetings to tell people about our culture, our religion, our history. Next month I'll go too. We'll change people's thinking. In time even the rowdies will give over their prejudices. Correctly informed, they'll see that Jews have always been good Germans, contributing to the common heritage of Beethoven and Schiller."

"And Goethe," I added.

"I don't know," Mother said, "whether everyone in Germany is as reasonable as you are, Günther."

"They are! Isn't reason part of the German heritage? Wasn't our government founded on principles of reason? Why must Hitler hang out in a flyspeck village in Bavaria? Why does the government forbid him to speak in public? Because of the German respect for reason! The government knows he's crazy! Watch, soon Hitler and the other Nazi nuts will be in prison or deported."

Günther glanced at Tante Ilse and, perhaps predicting her response, gave it himself. "Hitler," he laughed. "May onions grow in his belly!"

We stayed in Berlin three days. While Mother looked at apartments and met with shoe wholesalers, I filled my days with glorious sights. On our last evening we all went to the Deutsches Theater, where I wept over the romantic story of *Camille*. Afterward I was consoled in a café with cups of hot cocoa and pastries looming with alpine spires of whipped cream.

I was so impressed by the beauty and excitement of Berlin that on the night train back to Poland, my head swirled with images and I couldn't sleep. I thought joyously of my future, which I now knew had Berlin in it. And I thought daringly of a new idea. For as the train sped eastward, I realized Tante Ilse was wrong. I wouldn't make a very good seamstress. I would make a very good fashion designer. Maybe a great one.

ELEVEN

"Dora? Is that you on the line?"

"Of course it's me. When did you get back?"

"Yesterday."

"Then why didn't you come see me!"

"Dora, the telephone here is only for business." I was standing in our shoe store, and it was filled with holiday customers. "I can't talk now!"

"Too bad—I've got the best surprise!"

"Tell it quick."

"Don't be stupid! Surprises are no good on the telephone. I've got to tell you *in person*, so after work come to dinner."

Dora was about to hang up, but I quickly said, "This is our busiest time—we close late!"

"Come late then. 'Bye!"

All afternoon I measured feet and fetched shoes. Then after dark, when the last shopper was wished well, I hurried to Dora's house. Though I'd been away only a few days, we hugged like long-lost friends. She led me into the good room, where the cook had prepared a veal dinner for us on a tray. That's what I liked about Dora's house: Things were fancy.

I was bursting to tell her all about my trip to Berlin, but she was so wrapped up with her own talk, I couldn't get a word in.

"Lena, while you were in Germany, so was my father. He went to an auction in Frankfurt and guess, just *guess* what he bought me."

I hadn't a clue in the world what people bought at auctions, so I said, "A book?"

At this Dora laughed musically. "A book! Whatever would I do with it! Honestly, you know a book wouldn't be a big surprise!"

"A coat?" I said.

"Lena, sometimes you are a goose! Listen carefully, for here comes the surprise: My father went to Frankfurt and bought me"—Dora paused to increase my suspense—"an antique sleigh!"

If Dora had said her father bought her an antique carousel, I couldn't have been more surprised. I had never known any girl who owned a sleigh. Her very own sleigh.

"That's not all. Father got a certificate with it saying that it once belonged to a Russian princess. It's a *royal* sleigh!"

A royal sleigh. For a moment I was speechless at the wonder of it. Then I asked, "Where is it?"

"Still in Frankfurt, where it's being repainted. It'll arrive before the New Year, and Mother says I can ride in the sleigh on the night of Saint Sylvester."

The thought of riding on one of the most magical nights of the year in an antique sleigh, a sleigh once belonging to a *princess*, left me silent.

"It's very small," Dora continued. "It can seat only four. With our driver, Father, and me, there's room for just one more person."

"Perfect for your mother," I said.

Dora smiled, then kissed my ear as she whispered, "Mother hates the cold, so she said I should invite one of my friends, and Lena . . . I'm inviting you."

In the weeks that led up to the New Year, I was busier than ever. I had no time to dream of sleighs, moon over Berlin, or imagine my future. I was too busy even for films and cafés with the girls. I had sewn a skirt for Sala, but as I had no chance to see her, it hung in my own armoire. Our school had exams at this time, and how I passed them I don't know, for my head was buzzing with prices, style numbers, and customer names. Of course, it wasn't just I who was busy; all of Ledniezno was in a flurry. And each year it seemed the flurry started in a moment. One November moment. A sting in the air, an appearance of roof frost, a sudden sense of endings—then it would come—snow. Veiling our vision and bringing with it the inconvenience of muddy streets, wet wood, damp coats. It seemed in this moment, too, despite the apparent deadness of the season, there came a quickening. Our little town burst alive. In its center the marketplace swelled with shoppers from the villages, the estates, the farms. From all about gathered those who pinched pigs, weighed sheep, and blew the downy underfeathers of geese to discern plumpness. In the wintry air the stalls of the marketplace were jammed with cheap Christmas gifts, pine wreaths, and saint's day cards. The colorful kerchiefs, wooden toys, baskets of embroidered hankies, and red bags of gingerbread gave our winter market the look of a fair. And the vendors, like saints themselves, bowed over their warming pots of hot coals, waiting patiently for customers to decide, then—once choices were made— haggled like devils.

The shops on the street were no less busy. Despite the newspaper's urging not to buy from Jews, we had a good number of customers. We worked feverishly. For a whole week we came early to decorate the store. Stealing an idea I saw in Berlin, I persuaded Mother to cover the floor of our window with a length of white satin. Then on the cloth snowscape of valleys and hills (made by crumpled newspapers underneath) I placed pairs of our finest shoes, each pair encircled by green holly.

At this time of year the Freemasons' and Oddfellows' dances were held, and groups of girls hauling dresses crowded in to buy white satin pumps and to match colors for dyeing them. Ladies with money bought our French evening shoes. And for the thrifty we sold what Mother called "Miss Typist" shoes: practical black-strap pumps that could, when needed, be dressed up with bows. We sold children's shoes as gifts. These had to be wrapped in blue tissue with ribbons. And of course there came the annual families of peasants, for whom new shoes were prompted not by winter parties but by winter weather. We sold shoes for money, traded shoes for cider and cheese, and gave shoes away. Mother and I also packaged four dozen pairs of camel-hair slippers from Czechoslovakia, which we carried to the synagogue for distribution to the orphanage.

Then, just as suddenly as the flurry seemed to start, it stopped. Quiet set in. Like a great white pillow, the piling snow at last hushed our town. By early December the grumbling coal wagons, honking automobiles, churning autobuses, and creaking peasant carts were gone. In their place came swift sleighs. Wheels were replaced by runners, wagons converted to sleds. And with the change came the soft whoosh of snow and the polite jingle of harness bells.

The town bustle that began in November slowed. Liveliness went indoors. Whether around coal or more humble wood fires there came celebration. First Saint Martin's Day for feasting on goose. Then Saint Catherine's Day for dancing and Saint Andrew's Day for fortunetelling. About this time came our Jewish festival, Hanukkah, for lighting of candles and games of spinning the dreidel. And during Hanukkah—or sometimes after—came Christmas Eve, which the Poles called Wigilia. Christmas followed and, soon after, New Year's Eve, which we all celebrated and called Saint Sylvester, the night of new beginnings.

On Saint Sylvester the snow fell steadily all day. As we did every year, we rose early. Mother lit our coal oven, and I laid empty sugar sacks all around the kitchen. She heated oil in the big copper cauldron and fried the New Year's doughnuts, which she had filled with her own homemade plum jelly. When the doughnuts were golden, she lifted them out of the hot oil and set them on the sacks to drain. Then I sprinkled the doughnuts with powdered sugar that swirled in the air so that it seemed as if it were snowing indoors too. As we worked, every now and then Mother would look out the window and say annoying things. "You'll catch your death of cold tonight if you don't dress warmly," or "I don't know what Herr Gerhardt is thinking, taking children out in this weather!" or "I can't understand why you girls want to go for a sleigh ride in the dead of night!" Mother hadn't forbidden me to go, but her comments irritated me. Wasn't I sixteen years old? Did she think I was foolish enough to go outside without my coat? Did she think people actually froze to death in royal sleighs?

To all Mother's remarks I said nothing but just counted the hours until ten, when Dora would arrive for me. I was ready well before the time, and the second I heard the bell, I flew to open the door.

"You're as bundled as a baby!" Dora laughed when she saw me in my blue wool coat, knit hat, scarf, and mittens. Dora was dressed like a princess—all in white. White rabbit coat, white boots, white fur muff, white fur hat that now glistened with snowflakes. "Come, Lena. When you see my sleigh, you'll die of envy!"

"I hope not," I said, "for then how could I ride in it?"

Dora giggled just as Mother came in. She greeted Dora warmly, then turned to me. "When you get home, don't come up the front way. Go through the cellar and leave your muddy snow boots there. I'll put your slippers just inside the kitchen door, so you can come into the house without dirtying the rugs."

I was *so* embarrassed that right in front of Dora, my mother talked to me as if I were a child—just because the previous week I had accidentally tracked mud onto the rug and the spots had to be cleaned with sauerkraut juice.

"Yes, Mother," I said, not masking my annoyance. "I'll come in through the cellar. *Now* can we go?" I asked sarcastically. Mother gave me a stern look, for I was being rude. But as she said nothing, I quickly kissed her cheek, Dora sang good-bye, and we were out the door and down the stairs.

In front of the entryway of our house stood two fine black horses harnessed to a sleigh that seemed to have slipped out of a folktale—a shiny red sleigh with giant snowflakes stenciled in gold leaf on the sides, dark polished wood runners, large brass bells attached to the harness, and curling around the back of the blue tufted leather seats, a thick brass rail gleaming like gold.

As soon as he saw us, the driver got out and opened

the brass-handled door while Dora's father called cheerily, "Get in, my dears, get in." We climbed into the backseat, and handsome Herr Gerhardt, with his blue eyes and black mustache, turned to us from the front seat to make sure we spread the bear rug over our laps, advising us to tuck the ends under our bottoms so we'd stay covered. Then, at the driver's quick slap of the reins, we slid down the street as if on a silk ribbon.

TWELVE

We slid right out of town. Past the station yard, Herr Gerhardt's granary, the gasworks, slaughterhouse, artillery garrison, and cavalry garrison. It had stopped snowing, so the air was now bright and brittle. A full moon rode quickly through the clouds, and beneath it Dora's little sleigh raced across the earth. Having no wheels, we were not confined to roads but free to travel in any direction. Like a fairy's chariot our sleigh flew over meadows, frozen marshes and ponds. We sailed under the snowy boughs of oak and pine trees, the bells making merry music as we went.

Dora and I were ecstatic. What a feeling it was! The rush of cold air stung our cheeks, and every now and then we'd let out little bursts of laughter or squeals of delight. Under the blanket we squeezed each other's hands to further share our joy.

I had no idea where we were going—if anywhere at all. But after half an hour or so, and after passing along wide white fields deserted of herds and flocks, we stopped at a small farming settlement.

"Why are we stopping here?" I asked Dora.

"Every Saint Sylvester Papa brings brandy to his foreman's family," she explained.

Like ghosts that can arrive out of nowhere, shadowy figures suddenly appeared. In the dim light of their lanterns three peasant men approached the sleigh. The one whose pipe bowl glowed red in the dark talked obsequiously in broken German to Herr Gerhardt, thanking him for his generosity. The man instructed the others to remove the case of brandy, which I now realized was at Herr Gerhardt's feet. As Herr Gerhardt climbed out of the sleigh for this task to be accomplished, the pipe-smoking man asked him whether we might honor his home with a visit by the fire and a glass of hot rum punch.

Immediately, Herr Gerhardt said no. I was not surprised, for despite his kindness to me, he was an arrogant man. He might very well bring gifts to his workers, yet Dora's father was not one to socialize with peasants—and Polish peasants at that.

But Dora, who loved all novelty, pleaded for the visit. "Father, it would be terribly amusing to go inside. Please, can't we?" Herr Gerhardt, irritated by his daughter's request, quietly told her that no, it was not going to happen. However, Dora had a knack for turning people around, and now she used it. "Father," she said petulantly, "it's really too much to make us endure such a freezing ride without anything hot to drink. We're so very cold, we're shivering and we might get sick!" Under the bear rug we were warm as waffles, but Dora's self-pitying words had their effect. Reluctantly Herr Gerhardt agreed to a visit in the peasant's home—if it was kept short.

Our driver took us down a row of very small wooden houses. He stopped at one and we all got out. Then he steered the sleigh to the barn so he and the horses wouldn't have to wait in the cold.

"Welcome! Welcome!" our host, Pan Rudnik, crowed as he bade us enter. The one-room home smelled of forest and ripe grain and was warmed by a crackling fire. All about the room sat his family: his stout wife, an old woman, some young farmers, and children. In the back corner sat four young women with colorful ribbons in their braided hair. I saw one rise and exit through a narrow door.

It was a primitive but cheery home, hung with crosses and made festive for the season by straw mobiles studded with apples.

Dora and I took off our coats and hats, and as we did, we were much stared at. A girl of about eight stroked Dora's muff as if petting a kitten. The old grandmother, who had fewer teeth than a toddler, cheerily examined us. The young women looked at us with wide eyes and shy smiles as they served us animal-shaped cakes and glasses of hot punch. I spoke Polish in the store, so with a heart sting understood when I heard one of the women whisper to another, "Two sisters, one beauty."

Dora, who knew only German, did not catch this comment.

We sat on a long wooden bench drinking and eating and enjoying the strange newness of being in a peasant's home. Herr Gerhardt sat stiffly at the oak table, sipping a glass of brandy with his jovial host. He tried to appear friendly, but he looked pained to be entertained in a room in which babies howled, wash was hung, and under the stove chickens pecked at potato peels.

"MAY MY WORDS BE STRONG AND RESONANT, STRONGER THAN STEEL AND STONE!
THE KEY TO MY WORDS IS IN THE HEAVENLY HEIGHTS
AND THE LOCK IN THE DEPTH OF THE SEA."

We must have been in the house no more than five minutes when we heard this sudden, loud singing that seemed to come from behind the narrow door. Dora and I glanced at each other and immediately fell to giggling.

"Divination," the old woman explained to us.

"Divination?" asked Herr Gerhardt. "I thought you people do your fortunetelling on Saint Andrew's Day?"

The old woman sent him a toothless grin, then replied in broken German, "Yes, but whole of sacred season brings omens." Herr Gerhardt did not reply to her comment, so the woman, perhaps thinking she needed to explain, continued in a raised voice, "Appearance of cherry twigs on Saint Catherine's Day, direction slippers point on Saint Andrew's, sighting of stars on Saint Lucy's—they are holy omens that can predict future. But, sir—" and here the woman raised her voice even more—"omens of Saint Sylvester are greater than all! Only tonight—night of year's death—prophecies *cannot* be false!"

The old woman spoke with such conviction, I'm sure Herr Gerhardt wanted to say something like "Ridiculous rubbish!" But he checked himself and said nothing. Then the old woman turned to us and asked slyly, "Perhaps young ladies would like to see their future?"

At that Herr Gerhardt put his glass down, stood up, and said insincerely, "We have had a charming time, yet I'm afraid we must go."

"I'd love to get my fortune told!" cried Dora. "Oh please, Father, can't we? I've never had it done. Never!"

Herr Gerhardt had the look of a man who sensed his own weakness but felt compelled to appear firm. "We Germans are not a superstitious people," he said stiffly.

"But it's just for *fun*," Dora argued.

"No," said her father.

"Yes!" said Dora.

"No," said her father.

"But I'm sure," Dora said loudly, casting her lovely brown eyes on our host, "Pan Rudnik would think us very discourteous to leave so abruptly for no urgent reason."

As Pan Rudnik and his family were observing this exchange with great interest, Herr Gerhardt was trapped. He knew that to leave now after Dora's showy comment would indeed appear impolite.

"All right," he said miserably, "but we must leave soon."

The old woman led us to the door in the corner. Going through it, we found ourselves in a small washroom where a crude table had been placed against the splintery wall. On the table a candle burned next to a tin basin of water. The young women followed us in and stood around this table. Despite their gay ribbons they looked somber in the dim light. I got a shivery feel at the dark weirdness of it and suddenly wished Dora's father had not given in.

"Come," the old woman beckoned to us. "Don't be bashful!"

We approached the table. "Take off something of value," she commanded, "and place in the water."

Dora, who always wore a pretty sapphire ring, now tossed in her ivory hair barrette. "Put your *ring* in," I told her.

"I can't," she said airily. "I'm not wearing it."

"Hair trinkets work just fine," the old woman assured her. Then she turned to me, and rather embarrassed, I said, "I'm not wearing any jewelry or any hair clips."

"You have *something*," the woman said. I didn't think so, but as she said it so firmly, I felt around in my dress pocket and surprised myself by drawing out a pfennig left over from my trip to Germany. I tossed the coin into the basin.

As soon as it hit the water, the old woman shut her eyes and sang:

"COME FROM FOREST!
COME FROM FIELD!
COME FROM BARREN MOUNTAIN PEAK!
BRING MYSTIC VISIONS FROM AFAR
THAT THESE YOUNG MAIDENS SEEK!"

She sang so loudly and with such force that Dora and I stood transfixed. From all corners of the earth the woman summoned demons, and I translated her Polish words into German for Dora. But as the song went on, it became more complicated and finally incomprehensible. At last the old woman stopped, and we all watched as she moved her hands wildly over the basin. She picked up Dora's barrette and sang in a language I had never heard. All the while her arms gesticulated madly, making freakish shadows on the wall. I don't know how she knew where Dora was, for her eyes were still closed, yet she grabbed Dora's hand and intoned:

"YOU WILL MARRY—
WITH A FAIR AND DARING MAN OF FIGHT!"

Next she pulled out my coin, took my hand, and crooned:

"YOU WILL TARRY—
WITH A RARE AND CARING MAN OF FLIGHT!"

She held my hand so tightly, and Dora looked so puzzled by the old woman's Polish rhymes, that even though I tried hard not to, I giggled. This set Dora off, and in a moment we were simultaneously giggling and covering our mouths to control ourselves. The young women stared at us.

"Playful darlings," the old woman cackled. "Playful darlings."

Then, ending her divination ritual, she sang again, banishing the demons she had summoned:

"GO YOU NOW FROM WHERE YOU CAME!
REMOVE YOURSELVES FROM HERE.
FLEE FAST! FLY NOW!
ABANDON US, AND TAKE WITH YOU OUR
    FEAR!"

There came a silence after this song that was rudely broken by the sudden opening of the door.

"Mein Gott!"

We jumped at the voice. Herr Gerhardt stood in the doorway, staring at his gold pocket watch with exaggerated shock. "Eleven fifteen! *Mein Gott!* We must go!"

Dora and I hurried out of the washroom. We said hasty good-byes to the family as they stood on the porch calling back New Year's greetings: *"Dosiegu roku!*" they sang to us at the open door, and "*Szezwsliwego Nowego roku!*"

I taught Dora to respond, "*Nawzajem!*" "Same to you!" and we shouted this back, giggling all the while we climbed into the sleigh.

Fascinated by the old woman's prophecies, we were in high spirits on the way back. Our minds made fanciful images of our sweethearts, and we told them gaily to each other as we rode.

That night I felt wildly happy, for the frosty world seemed touched with magic. The moonlight colored the snow blue and made it twinkle as if with stars, so I had the enchanted feeling we were gliding across a vast mirror reflecting the sky.

After a while the driver stopped before a pond. Being cautious, he got out with the lantern to test whether it was frozen enough to cross. I looked around. We were stopped at the edge of the forest. From the sleigh it appeared a fairyland. I commented how mysterious it looked, and before I could stop her, Dora said, "Father, Lena and I want to get out. May we please for just a moment?" Herr Gerhardt turned to us. He gave a parental sigh and I saw his tired face was red with cold, yet he said, "I suppose while the driver is checking the ice, you may get out, but for no more than a few minutes!" Dora and I jumped out of the sleigh and walked a short way into the forest. We went in among a grove of pine trees whose frosty moonlit trunks shone like polished silver.

Suddenly Dora gripped my arm. "It's tonight, isn't

it?" she asked breathlessly. "It's on *this* night that people believe it happens!"

I knew what she meant. "I think so," I answered. "Yes, during the holy evenings—but only just before midnight."

Dora gripped my arm tighter. "It *is* just before midnight," she said. "It's *NOW!*"

A shivery thrill took hold of me, for many Poles believe that during the sacred season, the Earth changes and the laws of God and His world are changed. During this time, in these moments before midnight—only in these few moments—animals speak in human voices.

We stood listening, silent as the trees. Listening with our ears and our hearts too. Straining to hear. Hoping to hear.

"*Hooooooooo.*"

Dora screamed.

"Shhhh," I said, "it's only a wood owl hooting."

We were quiet once more, but I did not listen for talking animals. I listened to the eerie call of the owl, and through the trees I gazed at the softly glowing pearl that was the moon. In its light the dark shadows spread across the snow in intricate designs. Never had the world seemed to me so beautiful. That night I *felt* the meaning of the poem I so loved. I felt that night that everything on Earth was touched by God's holiness. The air and the land and the trees and the people and the animals and the leaves and the snow and each and every lowly stone, and I said aloud, " 'Are not even the rocks crowned with sacred shadows?' "

"What?" Dora asked.

"It's a line from one of Goethe's poems," I explained. "He's saying God's goodness touches everything. Everything."

"It's cold," Dora said. "Let's go back."

Detouring around the pond, our sleigh returned to Ledniezno. We arrived at midnight, and in every church at the same moment the bells tolled, so that as our horses trotted down Wlodoga Street, the whole town rang like a bell. The usually empty night streets were crowded with people celebrating. In the yellow light of the gas lamps they stopped to stare at Dora's royal sleigh with unbelieving eyes.

In a few moments we were in front of my building. I thanked Herr Gerhardt, wished him *"Gutes neues Jahr,"* then hugged Dora good-bye, her fur hat tickling my cheeks.

Stepping down from the sleigh was like waking from a dream. I hurried along the snowy pavement, then went carefully down the icy cellar steps.

The cellar was blacker than the night. It gave me a scary feeling to walk through it, and I had the urge to bolt straight to the stairs. But our cellar was so jammed with stored things, I was forced to go slowly. In my bulky winter coat I carefully went around the wicker baskets that held our Passover plates. Then in the blackness I began to maneuver past the wood boxes of sand in which our winter vegetables were buried. It was when I passed the last box that I heard it—a quick, scuffling noise! I froze. There was an animal near the coal bins. No doubt a rat! I had never been brave in the dark, and now the thought of being in blackness with a rat I couldn't see—a rat that might jump on me, or even bite me—filled me with fear. I waited. After several seconds of hearing nothing, I proceeded toward the steps. To calm myself, I slowly recited the names of our stored foods: "Pickled cucumbers, pickled carrots, pickled plums, canned potatoes, dried onions, pickled beets, pickled leeks, apples stowed in hay, milk curd, canned milk, cheese, dried figs, dried—"

"ACHOO!"

At the sound of the sneeze I froze again, but this time my heart pounded in terror. An animal sneezing with a human voice! I stood, still as death, listening. . . . When I detected human breathing, I knew. Somebody was in our cellar. Somebody who had been waiting to find me alone. And in the dark.

Thirteen

I bolted toward the stairs, but in my panic I stumbled over something—no—someone! We crashed into each other, and the two of us jumped back, screaming. The other person's scream sounded like my own; when I got my breath, I whispered, "Sala?"

I heard a soft whimpering and knew it was my friend. I reached out, grabbed for her arm, and pulled her up the stairs behind me. She moaned and sniffled all the way.

In the dark kitchen I yanked off my boots and hers as well, then fired off questions. "What are you doing here! Why are you hiding in our cellar? How long have you been down there? What's going on!"

But Sala could not answer, she was trembling so

badly. Over her cotton blouse she wore only a thin sweater.

"You're not wearing a coat!" I exclaimed; then, pulling her along as if she were a naughty little sister, I led her up to my room.

In the electric light Sala looked a pitiful sight. Her lips were blue with cold and her hair wet with snow. I helped her take off her clothes. They were appalling. Sala's skirt was the ghastly pink color of faded red cloth. When I took her dingy blouse and grayish socks to lay over the chair, I saw they were cold and clammy, as if her fear were so strong, it had spread to her clothes.

I pulled two flannel nightgowns from my dresser and handed her my blue one, which she pulled jerkily over her head.

Then we both got into my bed to warm ourselves, and as I stroked her tangly, damp hair, I whispered, "Why are you here?"

Her teeth were chattering so much that words could not come out, but after a few minutes my featherbed warmed her and she said in a faint voice, "Frau Gerhardt is very angry at me."

"Frau Gerhardt, angry at you? Whatever for?"

"She thinks I took Dora's sapphire ring."

"You're imagining things again!"

"No!" Sala protested. "Frau Gerhardt said so herself. She said I must have stolen it!"

"Tell me."

"Dora's ring is a little too big," Sala began. "At our first lesson I saw that when it turns around, the sapphire clacks on the keys, so I asked Dora to take it off when she plays. Now she's in the habit of removing it and placing it on the piano. When the lesson's over, she puts it back on. But after I left last week, Dora couldn't find her ring. Then, when I went to give her another lesson yesterday, Frau Gerhardt met me at the door and demanded the ring!"

At this memory Sala began to cry. Still stroking her hair, I asked, "Didn't you tell Dora's mother you don't know where the ring is?"

"Yes! But she wouldn't believe me! She said there was no one but me in the good room that day, so who else would have taken it? She said if I gave the ring back, she'd say nothing. But if I didn't give it back, she'd go to the police!"

Sala was sobbing now. I tried to comfort her. "Dora knows you wouldn't take the ring! Surely she'll say something to her mother to help you."

"It was Dora!" Sala cried. "It was *Dora* who told her mother that it was most likely me who took it!"

"Dora may be snobbish," I said, "but she's not evil, and saying that is evil! Besides, why would she even want to say it?"

"She's not good at the piano," Sala said, sniffling.

I almost laughed. "That's not a motive."

"Well," Sala went on weakly, "she doesn't like taking piano lessons, so . . ."

"So you think this is her way of ending them?"

Sala nodded.

"Dora wouldn't blame you just to end her lessons," I explained, "and anyway I doubt Dora's mother would believe such a ridiculous charge. I know Frau Gerhardt. She's smart."

"Dora has a way of *making* people believe her," Sala said with emotion. "But I can't make people believe me at all! They'll never *never* believe me over her!" Sala began to weep again.

Her words made me uneasy, yet I clung to my belief.

"Dora is my dear friend," I said. "Tomorrow you and I will go to her house and I'll speak for you. I'll tell both Dora and her mother that you're not a thief. You'll see," I promised, trying to make my voice cheerful. "They'll realize how wrong they were and we'll have a good laugh. Tomorrow there'll be apologies all around."

I didn't know whether Sala was listening to me. It was a long time before she stopped crying. Her sobs unnerved me, for despite my own words, I began to see truth ebbing into hers. I had to admit Dora was persuasive, but worse, her mother was a powerful woman. With her wealth and influence Frau Gerhardt could blaze a short trail from suspicion to sentence. Sala was crying so hard, the pillow was soaked. I stroked her hair for a long while until she calmed a bit and at last seemed to be sleeping. Then, because I was exhausted, I too fell asleep.

The next morning I woke late. Sala was not in the bed, and when I glanced over to my chair, her clothes were gone. But there was a note scribbled on a crumpled scrap of paper plucked from my wastebasket.

There won't be apologies. I've seen Frau Gerhardt's eyes. She'll tell the police. She said she will. She will.

I raced downstairs. Since it was New Year's Day, Mother had made our breakfast especially nice with jelly doughnuts and hot cocoa in our pewter mugs. She was hosting a coffee-klatsch this afternoon for a few elderly ladies from the synagogue, and I saw she was in a good mood.

"You must tell me all about the royal ride," she said teasingly. "Perhaps you girls met two handsome princes?"

I ignored her question, blurting out, "Did you see Sala?"

Mother's puzzled expression gave me the answer, and without explaining, I ran upstairs, threw on my clothes, and dashed out the door.

It was a fear that propelled me to Sala's home . . . but a fear of what exactly, I didn't know. I reached her apartment quickly. At the foot of the rusty stairs so much slushy snow was piled up, I got my legs wet above my boots. I knocked on the door of Sala's apartment several times, but there was no answer. It did not make sense. Surely, I thought, her family would be home on such a cold holiday morning.

Then, just as I turned to leave, the door was opened by an old woman wearing a ragged apron. She spoke only Yiddish, so I followed what she said with difficulty. She was saying something about Sala's mother being very ill and taken away to be cared for by a friend. I thought she also said that she herself was a neighbor who had come to care for the little boys. The woman seemed worried about Sala, for she had not seen her for two days. I tried to assure the old woman I would find her.

With my skirt freezing wet against my legs and my heart hammering, I hurried to Dora's house. When I reached her front door, I remembered that Dora's parents would most likely be entertaining visitors today for the New Year. This was confirmed for me when the door opened and I saw Hedwig wearing her formal, lace-trimmed uniform. Waiting in the hallway, I could see through the beveled-glass doors the small group of grown-ups chatting in the good room. I certainly didn't want to annoy Frau Gerhardt by interrupting her party. In fact I didn't want to deal with her at all if I could avoid it, so I was relieved when Dora came down the hallway to greet me.

"You look hideous!" she exclaimed. "Your boots are soaked and your hem's all wet!"

"Listen Dora, we've got to find Sala. Did she come here this morning?"

"Why would *Sala* come here?"

I don't remember what words I said next or in what order I said them, but I poured out my fear in one great rush. I told Dora how I found Sala in my cellar last night, how frightened she was, how terrified! I tried to explain how scared Sala was of Dora's mother going to the police, how bad that would be—not just for Sala, but for Sala's family.

"Please," I said, "could you and your mother please

tell Sala it was all a silly misunderstanding? When I find her, will you tell her today, please!"

"But it's no misunderstanding," Dora said. "Sala stole my ring. I'm sorry for her, but it was her choice to steal it."

I stared at Dora in disbelief, then said, "You don't know what you're saying! You can't honestly believe that Sala would take your ring! Sala's not a thief, and besides she doesn't care a fig for jewelry! She's terribly upset, and she's so strange—you know how . . . how *different* she is—I'm afraid she might do something stupid!"

"She already has," Dora replied dryly. "She stole my ring."

Dora's indifference to Sala was one thing, but her indifference to my concern, her apathy to my impassioned words, was more than I could bear. Tears stung my eyes and I heard my voice catch as I said, "You've no proof that Sala took your ring, yet you accuse her! Don't you understand you could be wrong? Don't you understand how serious your charge is? Don't you believe what I am telling you? How can I make you see?"

My voice had risen, and suddenly I realized I could be heard in the good room. I lowered my voice to ask Dora my heart's question: "What about our friendship? Don't you believe *me*?"

Dora paused, then answered in words that echoed in my heart years afterward.

"It's not that I don't want to believe *you*, but I can't trust Sala. You know how poor she is—she has a good reason to take my ring. Besides, Father says most Jews really can't be trusted. I mean Jews have such a reputation for betrayal right now, that even though we're friends, Lena, like everyone else, I have to be careful."

I stared dumbstruck, and seeing my face, she added gently, "Oh Lena, you mustn't take all this personally!"

I stood there like a fool looking at her, not knowing at all how to respond, but Dora's face told me she didn't particularly care whether I understood her or not. In confusion I mumbled something about needing to go and started toward the door. As I did, I heard the glass doors to the good room open and Frau Gerhardt call Dora. I did not turn to greet Frau Gerhardt, nor did I wait for Hedwig to open the front door. I opened it myself and hurried out into the bitter air.

FOURTEEN

My only thought was to get home, to be with Mother. I'd know what to do then. I'd be able to think when I got home, and Mother would help me find Sala.

Preparing for her guests, Mother was neatly laying the serviettes on the table. "You were certainly rude this morning," she remarked when I entered. "Why did you dash out without even having your breakfast?"

"I'm sorry, but I had to find Sala."

"Why?" Mother asked distractedly as she got the cake plates from the sideboard.

"She's lost," I answered, then told Mother everything. I told her how I had found Sala in our cellar after the sleigh ride and how upset she was about Frau

Gerhardt's accusation. How she had slept the night in my room but had run off before I woke. I showed Mother the note and told her that Sala was not at her apartment. Then painfully I recounted my visit to Dora.

"I have to find Sala!" I told Mother. "She's out in this weather without a coat, and she's so scared!"

Mother often said I was melodramatic, tending to exaggerate, yet as I talked, it was she who grew extremely serious. Her cheerful New Year's face turned grave and she spoke with urgency.

"You're right. We must find Sala at once. Change into a dry skirt and let's go. Be quick!"

"But what about your coffee-klatsch? What about those ladies?"

"I'll telephone them. Come on. Be quick!"

I ran upstairs and changed. Mother threw on her coat and we were out the door, heading for our store. When we got there, she went straight to the telephone. It made me fearful to open the shop door and even to turn on the light. It was absolutely forbidden for shops to open on Christian holidays, and I was afraid someone might report us. As Mother made her calls, I nervously stood guard on the street to explain to passersby that we weren't really open.

Standing outside, I was chilled to the bone, but before long a small, tattered black coach fitted with pinewood runners skidded to a stop in front of our store, and I realized Mother had telephoned our rabbi. Rabbi Fried, a tall, gray-bearded Hungarian, sat up on the driver's seat. He looked somber and pale; his sidelocks spiraled down his cheeks, wispy and gray as swirls of dust. Next to him sat Goat Welmer, who also looked somber and who wore a too-large black winter coat and an old fur hat. My mother went up to them and in rapid, urgent speech all three discussed Sala. They repeated words like "foolish," "sensitive," "impulsive."

Mother opened the door of the coach and beckoned me inside, and then I understood that Rabbi Fried would help us find Sala by driving us about the town.

We traveled through the icy streets, passing taxis and private buggies carrying New Year's visitors. Rabbi Fried seemed to have his own itinerary of places to search. In the next hour we went back to Sala's apartment, searched the synagogue, inquired at the café, questioned several congregants, spoke to the stationmaster, and even interrogated Milosz, the simple street sweeper. Returning around and through the same streets, we got no closer to finding Sala. As the afternoon wore on, our search appeared useless, and the streets, dotted with revelers, lay about us in icy indifference. I remembered Sala's favorite poem:

For upon a bower I'll lay me down
And flee forever the indifferent town. . . .

All at once I felt unbearably sad. It was a sorrowful, heavy feeling—as if my heart were a boat slowly sinking. I opened the coach window and banged hard with my fist on the outside of the door.

"Stop! Stop!" I cried.

Rabbi Fried brought the coach to a halt. I opened the door and jumped out. "I think we should go to City Park," I shouted up at the two men. "She might be there!"

Rabbi Fried looked doubtful, and Goat Welmer said roughly, "The park is deserted. It's winter, or didn't you notice?"

Mother leaned her head out the window. "Lena," she said gently, "I doubt Sala would go to a frozen park."

I ignored Mother's comment and continued to plead to Rabbi Fried, "Please, we're so near the park now. Couldn't we just take a quick look? Please?"

"Where in City Park?" Rabbi Fried asked.

"I'd have to show you," I answered. "I'd have to sit up on the ledge."

Despite the skeptical look on Goat Welmer's face, Rabbi Fried agreed to search the park. I climbed up beside him.

We drove through the stone archway into City Park, but I could barely recognize the place. All the familiar sights were now buried under deep drifts of snow. A landscape so recently filled with flowers and birdsong lay barren and silent. Skeletal trees were the only life at all, and I tried to use them as markers.

"Go there," I directed Rabbi Fried. "Go on farther, now there, turn left, no right, go back, now turn right."

I hoped my directions were correct yet also hoped Sala would *not* be in this forbidding place. And so it was a hopeful, fearful exercise circling around and around the cold deserted paths.

Suddenly Rabbi Fried yanked back hard on the reins and brought the coach to an abrupt stop. Rabbi Fried, whom I had always heard talk in a gentle voice, now spoke severely to me. He ordered me to sit inside the coach with my mother so I wouldn't be chilled, as he and Goat Welmer would go on foot to search. I wanted to search too and would have protested had not his stern voice inhibited me.

Reluctantly I climbed inside the coach and sat next to Mother. I saw we were at the edge of what looked almost like a small glacier with a bony ash tree standing sentinel. Then, all at once, I realized my directions had been correct. This stark, shrouded place was our beloved Daisy Dell! From the coach window I saw Rabbi Fried and Goat Welmer walk purposefully there. Walk purposefully toward *something*.

Then in a flash I saw the distant patch of pink. Mother must have seen it as well, for she pushed my head toward her lap. But I pulled myself free in time to see that the patch on the snow was a motionless figure. To see Goat Welmer take off his greatcoat and, as tenderly as a father tucks in his child at nighttime, lay it over the body.

According to Jewish custom, Sala had to be buried by the next morning. The second of January 1928. I did not cry at the sudden ceremony, and in the months that followed I could not bring myself to visit her grave. But then later that year, after Sala's mother had moved back to Grajewo and after I had turned seventeen, I went to the Jewish cemetery.

I told no one, for I wanted to be alone. It was a bright autumn day. I walked slowly down the long rows of graves until at last I found Sala's. I stood before her grave, reading her name and the dates on a marker, awed by the strange fact that I was now a year older than her.

For a long time I stared dumbly at the grave, feeling awkward. I know I should have prayed, but instead I knelt and began to pull at the weeds growing around the tomb, and as I did, the grief I had held inside came out at last. I broke into sobs. I cried for my friend and the life she would never have, and I cried for me too. Curling up on Sala's grave as if it were my bed, I wept for us both.

Then, after a while, I remembered Mother once saying that at a cemetery you should never look down but up—to be lifted. So I stood, wiped my eyes, and looked up toward Heaven. Where the unplayed songs of the dead are God's music.

FIFTEEN

1929–1932

Dora and I did not speak to each other. Our estrangement was painful while we were in school, but by the end of 1928 I had dropped out of school anyway. The problem was that the Higher German Daughters' School began supporting the National Socialist German Workers' Party—the Nazis. The growing Nazi sympathies of my classmates and teachers soon made it impossible for Greta and me to attend school. This became clear to me one day during class.

We were reading a selection of poems in a new German textbook. We came to one poem that we recited together as in a chorus. It was a famous poem by the great German poet Heinrich Heine, and it was a very familiar poem, for we had read it in the lower grades on several occasions. The book gave the title of the poem, "The Lorelei," but underneath were the words "Author Unknown." Convinced there had been some printing error, I raised my hand and asked our teacher why Heinrich Heine's name wasn't beneath his poem. Having studied at the University of Munich, Herr Detmold was a literate man, yet he answered stiffly, "The author is unknown."

"But Herr Detmold, we read this poem last year," I argued. "You yourself taught us that it was by Heinrich Heine!" I looked around the room for support, but the other girls stared down at their desks.

Then Greta raised her hand. "Lena is right," she said quietly. "*You* know Lena is right." Greta and I got two demerits for "impudently challenging authority." But that night when I went through the book at home, I saw that all poems by Jews were now captioned with the words "Author Unknown." In Heine's case it was even more absurd, for he was born a Jew but was later baptized.

Soon after the poem incident, when tuition for Greta and me was tripled, we dropped out of the school. Then Thea and Birgit and almost all the remaining German families we knew moved to Germany, and after a few months the Higher German Daughters' School closed.

There was a Polish high school for girls in Poznań, but it didn't welcome Jews. In Warsaw and some of the villages there were Jewish schools, but they were far away, instruction was in Yiddish, and their diplomas were not recognized by the state. Some Jewish girls my age went to schools run by Zionists, those who wanted to make a Jewish homeland in Palestine. I might have liked these schools, for they taught Jewish history, agriculture, and Hebrew, but Mother had no liking for Zionists, whom she thought foolish idealists with dangerous ideas. So, with no education options, I spent hours alone at my sewing machine, creating clothes of high style.

In 1929 I became an assistant to the best seamstress in town, Pani Poyarska. Pani Poyarska was a kind, intelligent woman who taught me the most intricate and complex design techniques. Every now and then she let me have free rein to design clothes for some of her customers. Of course she could not tell them that it was *I* who designed the clothes or they might not have bought from her.

By now there existed throughout Poland a tacit boycott of all Jewish businesses. On the radio and in the newspapers Poles were encouraged to do business only with Polish Christians. *"Swoj do swego!"* "Stick to your own kind!" was a battle cry that had become louder. Our faith in Pilsudski was shattered. It seemed that the growing success of the German Nazi party had made anti-Jewish sentiment more acceptable in Poland, and Pilsudski had allowed Parliament to make the boycott a national duty. The economic boycott left most of the three and a half million Polish Jews in poverty and us near bankruptcy. Yet though we had far fewer customers than the previous year, and though now we could barely pay our bills, Mother insisted we stay in business.

At eighteen I had only one remaining friend, Greta,

and we were so bored, we would see the same films again and again. My present was dull and my future unpromising. So in the late summer of 1930 I confronted Mother.

She and I were in the stockroom of our store, taking inventory. On this hot afternoon we had been working on the inventory for hours, and the stockroom was warm and stuffy. I was up on the ladder, noting down style numbers from the shoe boxes. As I worked, I felt unsettled. The heat combined with my nervousness made me feel as if at any moment I'd jump out of my skin. Suddenly I exploded in anger. "WHY DO WE STAY HERE? I HATE IT HERE! I HATE IT!" I hurled a box of shoes to the floor to punctuate my rage.

"Come down from the ladder and we'll talk." Mother spoke calmly, but I saw from her face that my outburst shocked her.

I came down from the ladder but could not stop my emotion. "Why do we have to live among people who despise us?" I cried. "Why? For what are we sacrificing our lives? It's been three years since you promised we would move to Berlin. Three years! You *promised* we'd move, but every year you say, 'Perhaps next year.' If I can't live in Germany, how will I become a fashion designer? How? How will I get an education? How will I find a husband? How will I have a life if I don't go to Germany?"

I was crying now, for I was so miserable, so bored, so lonely. I sat on the floor, not caring what Mother thought, and gave way to self-pitying grief.

Mother perched on one of the ladder steps and said quietly, "It's true that I've put you off about our moving. It's not that I didn't want to take you away from here. But now is not the time to go."

"Why not? We could leave everything! Just leave it all and go to Germany. We could start over! If we could just live in our Fatherland, I'd work hard for us!"

"You don't know what you're saying," Mother said in a quiet voice, trying to calm me. "You've read Günther's letters, so you should understand that this is not a good time. With the Depression, two and a half million Germans are out of work. The streets and parks seethe with the unemployed. By promising them work, the Nazis have gained a lot of power. They had only twelve seats in Parliament, yet just this week they won one hundred and seven! Nazi sympathy is growing fast; this is not the time to move to Germany."

"So?" I asked. "When is the time?"

"When the Nazi fad is over. It will run its course quickly, but in the meantime we must have faith that life will get better, both here and in Germany. Wisdom will prevail soon, but now we must wait."

Wait. I despised the word. Wait. It meant tedium and weakness and automatic obedience. Wait. A cold, damp, dishrag word. A gray word, limp and powerless.

"I don't want to wait! Let's go anywhere!" I begged. "Jewish boys who aren't allowed in Polish universities go to schools in Czechoslovakia. Why don't we go there? Or France? What about Holland? What about America!"

"We can't just go anywhere we please," Mother answered. "Without relatives in another country, it's nearly impossible to get visas."

"*Nearly* impossible is not impossible," I countered.

"But, Lena, even if we could get visas, we'd still need money, not just for the voyage but for living."

"Then let's sell the store," I said.

"We can't," Mother answered. "We'd never get what we paid for it. Not in these times."

"So what," I said. "We could arrive somewhere poor and *make* money."

Mother looked at me as if I were a simpleton. "How can you make money if you don't know the language! Who would hire you? Be realistic, Lena. Right now we have no place to go."

To my mind Mother was rigid and wrong, so I said the words that at last made her angry. "If we were Zionists, we'd have a place to go."

The word *Zionists* was out of my mouth no more than a second when a slap landed hard across my cheek. "Don't ever mention that word again! When you say the word *Zionist*, you might as well say *outlaw*! You might as well say *Communist*! You might as well say *traitor*!"

I reeled back from the slap. I was in a kind of shock, for Mother had never slapped me before. My eyes stung with tears and I turned from her in humiliation. Our conversation was over, and for the rest of the afternoon we worked in silence. As I worked, I tried to understand how Mother and I had come to this. I knew only a little about Zionism. But I knew to be a

Zionist—to even talk of Jews creating their own country in Palestine—was believed by many Jews to be sacrilegious, dangerous, even mad. Rabbi Fried had often preached against what he called "idealistic madmen." Yet I also knew that Zionism was growing rapidly, sweeping up the young Jews of Poland. Thousands went passionately to Zionist meetings, often in secret, and wore their blue-and-white *blau-weiss* pins inside their clothes.

Mother's slap told me something that words could never have. I had gone too far. I had broken some family belief. I didn't understand it completely but felt I was wrong, and I vowed that from now on I would control my emotions as well as my talk. Above all, I would never speak of Zionists again.

As the months passed, we had so few customers that Mother and I alternated working in the store alone. One afternoon in April I was there by myself. Mother had gone home to prepare dinner, and I had come in to complete the inventory when I heard the bell jingle over the door. I went to greet the customer and saw it was a boy—a young man, really. I guessed him to be a year or two older than me, perhaps twenty-one. He was tall and athletic with thick, dark hair curled by the wind. He was the most handsome boy I had ever seen in my life. I could easily have stared at him forever, but I was so shy I could barely meet his large blue eyes. Had Mother been there, I would have persuaded her to wait on him while I finished the inventory, but as I was now the only one in the store, I asked, "May I help you?"

"I want to buy hiking boots," he said. Out of courtesy he spoke to me in German. His voice was strong, and he had a refined Polish accent. I figured he was most likely brought up on one of the wealthy Polish estates.

"What is your size?" I asked.

"I'm not sure. I suppose we'll have to measure my feet, won't we?" He smiled. I measured his foot, disappeared into the stockroom, took a deep breath, and luckily found we had Austrian hiking boots in his size.

Mother would have been horrified to see how I merely handed him the box of boots rather than lift them out, praise their features, then fit them on his feet and lace them up too. But I was tongue-tied and my hands felt clumsy.

"What do you think?" he asked after he'd laced them up and was walking about the carpet. "Do you think they'd be good for hiking?"

"I . . . I don't know," I answered stupidly. "I've never been hiking."

"Never been hiking! That's a shame. A terrible shame. You might as well say you've never been breathing."

"Why?" I asked.

"Because it's just the greatest thing there is, that's all."

"Why?"

"Because when you hike to a mountaintop, you can feel the clouds," he explained. "You're far above the world on a mountaintop . . . so far above . . . you can smell the sky."

I smiled. "Is it really that wonderful?"

"It is. In the mountains the air is pure. And when I climb higher and higher through the clouds, it sometimes feels as if I'm marching toward Heaven, as if I could hike right off the Earth." He stopped, looking suddenly a bit shy himself. "I'm not explaining it well," he said. "I just know I like it."

While he was talking, he was walking around and around, testing his boots, alternately looking down at them and looking at me. As he circled me, I marveled at how blue his eyes were, how tanned his skin. And the way he spoke! With such energy and joy. How I wished Jewish boys could talk like that! I thought, but instead said, "You make hiking sound holy." To my utter amazement, he answered:

"Nothing's outside that's not within,
For nature has no heart or skin.
All at once that way you'll see
The sacred open mystery."

"You know Goethe?"

He grinned. "Doesn't everyone?"

I wrote up the sale on the receipt slowly, as if I wanted him never to leave the store. Yet after I handed him his boots, he was the one who lingered.

"Do you like poetry?" he asked, his eyes locked on mine.

I loved it more than anything yet answered only, "Sometimes."

I looked down flustered, and when I looked up again, he smiled and I saw his teeth flash strong and white.

After he left, I stood at the side of the window and watched him cross the street.

That evening I did not feel well. My face felt hot, and when I sat down to supper, I could not eat. I did stupid things too. I put my dirty plate in the bread box and the bread loaf in the sink. Mother pulled the ruined bread out of the dishwater and looked at me with concern. "You're not well. Go to bed—you need rest."

I went to my room. In the dim light of dusk I lay on my bed but could not sleep. It seemed that everything was changed. *I* was changed. I felt a new kind of restlessness. I felt like crying one minute and laughing the next. I felt a yearning as I'd never known. I ached for impossible things. To *feel* the blueness of sky, to *feel* the blueness of his eyes, to hike with him. Right off the Earth.

Sixteen

Berliner Tageblatt
13 April 1931

SPECIAL REPORT BY GÜNTHER KATZ

Recently the Nazis led a parade from the Reichstag to the Leipziger Strasse. It was some parade! When they got to the Leipziger Strasse, they smashed the department store windows and attacked any bystander at all—anyone who they thought might be a Jew. This is just one example of what daily life in Berlin has become. Hate explodes anywhere. Street corners, cafés, cinemas, restaurants, dance halls. Day and night. Knives are pulled from pockets, fists strike out with spiked rings. Beer mugs are thrown, chair legs are broken off for truncheons, and guns slide out of holsters. With six and a half million supporters, the National Socialists are now the second-largest party in the Reich. Yet I respectfully urge our leaders to curb the violent behavior of the Nazis. If it is not checked, the democratic welfare of our country is at risk. Germany has an illustrious tradition of moderation, intellectual discourse, and reason that is now being threatened by right-wing extremists. . . .

I felt proud reading Günther's article. I admired the way he so seamlessly put words together. The sense of his words. The weight of them. Günther showed how anti-German the Nazis are. Mother is right, I thought. Günther has faith in our country. He has no tolerance for evil, yet he has forbearance. Reading Günther's article, I felt my own dissatisfied thoughts as selfish, impatient, gloomy. I would try, I thought, to be more hopeful, like Günther and Mother.

In my new resolve I sewed another Polish flag for our home. I wanted to make a grand one, as big as the flag on our town hall—a flag that could stretch the whole width of our balcony. And so, early on the 3rd of May, Polish Independence Day, I was at my sewing machine, putting the final touches on my flag.

As I worked, I mused how many people ignorantly made their flags in the wrong colors or unwittingly made the flag of Czechoslovakia! The Czechoslovakian flag being identical to the Polish one except that the red and white segments were reversed. It was absurd how many citizens were fined every year for flying the wrong flag on national holidays. Not me. I had made the perfect Polish flag, its dimensions precisely measured and its fabric and colors exactly matched to the official government flags.

I was nearly done when Mother came into the room to remind me to hang the flag by eight. "If you don't," she warned, "we'll be fined five zlotys. It seems each year the policemen check houses earlier and earlier!" Then she left in a hurry to hang the other flag at the shop. At ten to eight I finished the new flag, grabbed it, and rushed to the balcony. I secured either end with rope to the railing, and the flag unfurled itself smoothly and evenly. I ran downstairs to admire the effect from the street. It's beautiful, I thought. In the strongest sailcloth. Correctly designed. Professionally sewn.

At nine, people started to line the streets, and as soon as I heard the approaching music, I went to the balcony. All the way from Wlodoga Street came the parade. First rolled the trucks from the artillery garrison, bearing soldiers who saluted the crowd. Next came the cavalry garrison, trotting on horses wearing little Polish flags sprouting from their blinders. Then marched the World War veterans, some with graying mustaches and clinking medals. Behind the military, walking slowly as in a funeral procession, came the priests leading a brigade of choirboys who sang in girl voices too quiet for a parade. After them classes of schoolchildren waved cheekily to their parents with the paper flags they'd made, while their teachers walked behind them, arms linked. To the roar of the crowd and like a proud army itself, the soccer teams advanced, then the swimming teams and the wrestling teams, many of the young men winking at the women as they passed.

With important officials surrounding him, the mayor handshaked his way down our street while his wife and daughter, wearing corsages, rode alongside in an automobile. The bankers marched, boring everyone. The *Lech* newspaper staff marched, throwing free newspapers to the crowd. The postal workers marched with their own corps of fumbling trumpeters. The firemen rolled their three trucks solemnly down the street. And behind them the orphans marched with expressions of practiced gratitude. The Freemasons and Oddfellows marched, the potbellied tavern keepers marched, and perhaps strangest of all, the street sweepers marched, shouldering their scraggly brooms like rifles.

Because work was abandoned today, people were in a jolly mood. The crowds sang along with the band music and indiscriminately cheered everything. Peddlers wove among the crowd, selling pretzels, candy, small pictures of Jesus, of Mary, of the Polish flag, and of Marshal Pilsudski. But it was with the newspaper-wrapped packets of sunflower seeds that they really made their money. The seeds were popular not only for eating but also for use as a kind of confetti by the teenagers, who flung handfuls onto the marchers with cries of *"Jeszcze Polska nie zgineta!"* "Poland has not yet perished!"

I watched the parade as it passed underneath our

balcony and kept watching until it turned the corner with all the crowd following it, leaving my street littered and empty . . . or so I thought. For just then I saw across the street the very boy who had come into the store to buy hiking boots. Watching him, I lingered on the balcony too long, for when he glanced up, he saw me.

"Hello!" he called.

I waved, and then with mingled fear and pleasure I saw he was crossing the street to talk to me.

But after he crossed the street, the strangest thing happened. For several moments he just stood there gazing up at me on my balcony as if I were Juliet. He was either tongue-tied or transfixed, and his silence made me blush. To break the embarrassment of it, I said, "How are the boots?"

"Which boots?" he asked, teasing me.

"You know perfectly well which boots!" I answered.

"My boots are perfectly well, thank you. And yours? How are your *shoes* today?"

I laughed. He was funny.

"You look lovely when you laugh!" he called up. "But I think you don't laugh much, do you?"

It was true. I hardly laughed anymore. But how did he know? "I laugh all the time!" I called down to him.

"Then perhaps," he suggested, "we could laugh *together* sometime. Do you like Charlie Chaplin films?"

He was asking me for a date! This was not something I had expected, and I felt at once surprised and sad.

"I can't go out with you," I said.

"Why not?"

"I just can't. It'd be all wrong."

"Why? What would be wrong?"

He didn't understand how different our worlds were. "Everything would be wrong," I answered. "*Everything.*"

"Well," he said, looking embarrassed, "I guess *everything* covers it all, doesn't it? I'd better be going. *Auf Wiedersehen.*"

I stood on the balcony after he walked away, thinking—savoring his words, *You look lovely when you laugh*, and wondering why sometimes life seemed a cruel joke.

"JEW! TAKE DOWN THE FLAG!" I was about to go in when I heard the yelling.

"HOW DARE JEWS HANG OUR POLISH FLAG!"

Looking into the street, I saw four young men shouting up at me.

"TAKE DOWN THE FLAG! TAKE IT DOWN—OR WE'LL TEAR IT DOWN!"

Their chant made me furious! I was *not* going to take down the flag. Not only because it was against the law to take your flag down before sunset, but because I refused to show I was afraid.

"TEAR IT DOWN! TEAR IT DOWN! TEAR IT DOWN!" they hollered.

Common rowdies. Young thugs, most likely drunk. I ignored them, pretending not to hear. But when I turned again to go in, I saw out of the corner of my eye that one of them, nimble as an ape, was climbing up our drainpipe. As the others yelled, he made swift upward progress. Soon the roughneck would be high enough to reach the bottom railing of our balcony. If he got a foothold, it would be an easy leap over the railing, and a kick to the glass doors would give entry to our home. What could I do?

The hiker boy had gotten to the end of the street, and I was about to shout for him to get help but saw that was unnecessary. He had heard the loud rowdies, and turning back, he ran up the street until he was again beneath the balcony. He pulled hard at the left foot of the climber. He pulled so hard, the climber lost his balance, fell with a thud to the pavement, and lay there in pain. The three others leaped on the hiker boy, beating him mercilessly.

"BULLIES!" I screamed. But screaming was useless. I was nearly hysterical with fright, yet knew I had to do something fast!

I glanced around. Our balcony had five large flower-pots of geraniums, secured to the inside railing by round metal holders. I grabbed one of these heavy pots, tugged it up and out of its holder, and held it over the balcony. I had to be extremely careful with my aim. In a few seconds, when one of the attackers stepped back, I let fall the pot. I was aiming for the ruffian's head, but I missed. The pot struck his shoulder, bounced off, and crashed to the concrete. Still, the blow crippled him, and I breathed easier seeing that he could no longer fight.

My relief was short-lived, for though there were now only two opponents, each picked up a piece of broken pottery and held his jagged shard menacingly in front of the hiker. Right in front of his eyes!

"RUN!" I screamed to him. "RUN!" But instead of running, he stood there, poised to fight, his eyes darting from one attacker to the other like a trapped animal.

I grabbed another pot and was just about to let it fall when the attackers lunged. But the boy did something brilliant! As the two charged toward him, he ducked low and swapped places with them as if in a country dance. Then in one swift movement he scooped up two great handfuls of spilled soil, and as they lunged again, he flung it straight into their eyes and mouths.

As the hooligans cursed and spat, the boy won a few seconds' reprieve.

"HURRY!" I shouted to him. "RUN! THE BACK DOOR! ROUND THE SIDE! THE BACK DOOR! RUN!"

I dashed inside and leaped three steps at once down the stairs. I reached the back door that led into our laundry room just in time to pull him in. I slammed the door, locked it, latched it with the iron hook, grabbed his hand, and ran ahead to the next, inner door. I slammed, locked, and latched that one too. Two doors for safety! That was the beauty of our back entrance.

"They can bang all they want on the outside door," I assured the boy. "But they can't get in!"

They tried. Having abandoned climbing the gutter

pipe, they beat on the door with their fists and kicked it with their boots, all the time shouting vulgar things. Though I was certain they could not enter, I stood frozen in nervous silence until at last the terrifying noise stopped and I knew they had gone.

I don't know how long I stood there with this Polish boy in our laundry room. While the banging and yelling were going on, I did not even think how strange the situation was. But when it became quiet, I was suddenly and acutely aware that we stood in a very small dark room, extremely close together. And I was still holding his hand! I quickly let go of it, yet I was so close to him I heard his breathing as if it were my own. I smelled his sweat as if it were mine, and the blood that dampened his cheek seemed to wet my face too.

"I don't think I got your name," he said formally, as if we were at an elegant party.

"Lena," I said, "and you?"

"Janusz."

"A real Polish name," I remarked.

"Yes," he said vaguely.

I expected him to leave then, but instead he said, "That was wonderful, the way you dropped the flowerpot! Whatever made you think of it?"

"Mickey Mouse."

"Mickey Mouse?" He laughed. "You're joking!"

"No, it's true," I said, starting to relax. "I saw a new American cartoon last week. There was a cat standing at an open window trying to drop a flowerpot on Mickey Mouse . . . the scene came back to me."

Janusz laughed again. His laugh was warm and I laughed too, for dropping the flowerpot now seemed comical.

"Well, you had excellent aim," he said.

As he hadn't added "for a girl," I could afford to be modest. "I don't think my aim was good," I replied. "You see, I was aiming for his head."

"It's best you missed, then, or you might have killed him."

There was a pause; then I said, "That was pretty brave what you did. I mean the way you took on all four. And it was terribly clever to throw the soil into their eyes!"

"Some of it went into their mouths too," he said.

"Yes, and I'm so glad I use my father's secret soil-enriching ingredient."

"What's that?"

"Horse manure."

We both laughed again. I said, "I suppose there's no punishment for those bullies."

"They have sown the wind, and they shall reap the whirlwind," Janusz said. In Hebrew.

If he had spoken Chinese just then, I wouldn't have been more shocked.

"Are you a Jew?" I asked.

He grinned. "Isn't everyone?"

I was so surprised, I didn't answer. I didn't speak at all. The truth was I didn't want to say anything. All I wanted to do was stand there. I was aware of how good I felt standing there with him. The cool air of the washroom felt not just warm but charged with a kind of electricity. It was as if I could feel the very molecules of the air against my skin, and when he spoke I could reach out and touch the shapes of his words.

His cheek was still bleeding. I pulled my handkerchief from my dress pocket and dabbed his cheek gently, blotting up the blood. While I did so, I wondered what it was like to kiss a boy, but as I dabbed a spot of blood on his neck, I noticed it under his shirt collar. There it was, the tiny Zionist pin, the *blau-weiss* pin. And the sight of it chilled my heart.

SEVENTEEN

It was a mistake telling Greta about Janusz and the flag incident; she teased me mercilessly. "Isn't this new boy your hero!" she crowed. I understood her silliness, for like me she was bored; but why did she conjure up romance where it didn't exist? Thank God I hadn't told her about Janusz and me in the laundry room! She'd have tormented me.

Greta was really something. At first, with dear Sala departed, Birgit and Thea moved, and Dora estranged from both of us, we had only each other. But soon Greta got her sister to introduce her to some young Polish Jews, and she forged a dozen new friendships.

A few weeks after the parade, Greta announced,

"I'm organizing a picnic Sunday at noon. Come to the lakeside where the birches grow—your hero will be there."

"Janusz! When did *you* meet him? How?"

"Yesterday. Through someone who knows someone who knows him."

"Well, I'll come," I told her, "if you stop your ridiculous talk. Janusz was very brave, but he's not my hero. He's not my *anything*."

"All right, he's not your anything, but I'm glad I invited him; girls should have at least one gorgeous boy to look at . . . don't you think?"

"Looks aren't everything," I replied, a little too severely.

"Perhaps," said Greta with a smile, "but they do count for something."

———

HAIR: Brown and frizzy.
FACE: Oval.
SKIN: Pale but smooth.
EYES: Brown and big.
NOSE: Not big. Not small. Not classic.
MOUTH: Too wide.
CHEEKBONES: Not high enough.
OVERALL IMPRESSION: *Plain.*

Looking in the mirror, I regretted with all my heart that I wasn't beautiful. I walked back several steps to judge my figure. As I was nineteen now, I saw a woman's body. I took note:

NECK: Nice and long.
BUST: Figs, not peaches.
WAIST: Slender.
HIPS: Rounded but not too rounded.
LEGS: Shapely.
FEET: Small, arched.
HEIGHT: Not tall; not short.
OVERALL IMPRESSION: *Pleasing.*

Conclusion: As I couldn't show off my face, I should show off my figure. But how? I opened the armoire and appraised my six dresses.

Not one casual spring dress to wear, nor money to buy a new one. Not even material to *make* a new dress. With fewer customers now, I had to give up purchasing anything not absolutely essential. How I hated it! I sat on my bed feeling sorry for myself when my eye caught the cover of *Das Fräulein* magazine. Trousers. That was the new look. Trousers would be perfect for a picnic—if I had material to make them. I looked at the cover again. It showed a beautiful model in cream-colored muslin trousers with a matching muslin shirt. "Cool, Comfortable, and Classy," the caption read. I studied the photo for several moments, then hurried down to the kitchen and pulled from a drawer three clean flour sacks. By evening I had cream-colored muslin trousers. Cool, comfortable, and classy.

The next Sunday I made my way through the birch grove down to the bank of Lake Lipówka. I was carrying my picnic contribution: an apple cake. Greta introduced me to four girls and four boys, all friendly. As Germans, Greta and I had rarely socialized with Polish Jews, because their language and culture were so different. Yet now in this darkening time we grew closer, and the differences didn't seem to matter. We were in good spirits, talking easily in German, Polish, Yiddish, often changing languages in midsentence to aid understanding.

At that picnic I was happier than I had been in a long time. With only Greta as my friend I had been lonely, but that day I was with people my age again. It felt right. We laughed about a hundred things, and our conversations touched on books, films, travel. We told jokes, talked sports, sang new songs. Many Polish Jews were highly religious, but these young people were not. They were all worldly, modern, outspoken. The girls—Masha, Tova, Irena, and Sosia—were clever and down-to-earth. Masha, especially, was like no girl I had ever seen. She was tall and beautiful; her intelligent blue eyes looked at you deeply. Her skin seemed like suede, both soft and strong. She spoke seriously without the slightest shyness or hint of flirtation, and I envied her confidence. The boys—Kuba, Josef, Tadeusz, and Zygmus—were full of ambition. Not permitted into Polish universities, they were, all of them, off to other countries—to Czechoslovakia, to Romania, and the luckiest, the handsome Tadeusz, to Chicago, where his older brother lived. Tadeusz paid devoted attention to me, telling me all about the skyscrapers in America, asking my opinion on books, even discussing the benefits of sewing one's own clothes! I thought him exceptionally nice, since the few boys I had known talked mostly of their own interests. When Tadeusz smiled, his green eyes sparkled like the sunlit lake behind him.

"I'm hungry!" Greta complained. "I'm tired of waiting for Janusz. Where can he be?"

"You know Janusz," laughed Tadeusz. "He's probably running errands for his grandfather."

"Does his grandfather live with him?" I asked.

"No, the other way around. Janusz lives with his grandfather. He couldn't study architecture in Warsaw, so he came here to live with his grandfather, who was an architect in Czechoslovakia. Janusz is learning from him."

"Like having his own private tutor," I remarked.

"Exactly," Tadeusz replied.

"YES! WE HAVE NO BANANAS! WE HAVE NO BANANAAAAAAAAAAAAAS TODAY!"

Just as Greta was opening our food baskets, we heard this singing.

"Janusz!" we all cried, turning to the boy standing under the birch tree carrying a soccer ball and a bunch of bananas.

Smiling, Janusz strode up the bank, his dark curls lifting in the breeze. When he sat down, Greta scolded him for being late, handed him a plate, then much to my embarrassment introduced him to me in front of everyone by saying slyly, "And of course, you know the girl in the chic pajamas!"

"We've met," he said, throwing me a kind smile.

I smiled back politely, but inside I had a weird feeling—a kind of jittery joy.

As we ate, Lake Lipówka glittered with diamonds and the bright blue sky stretched over us like a silk banner. We feasted on herring, rye bread, hard-boiled eggs, bananas, and apple cake, all washed down with buttermilk. When we had our fill, the boys got up and kicked the soccer ball around as if they were all eight years old. When they tired of that, they took off their shirts and dove into the lake, splashing each other mercilessly. They tried to persuade the girls to come in, but as we hadn't brought our bathing suits, we just dipped our feet into the lake, shrieking with delight at its spring coldness.

At last we all returned to the bank and lazily talked. Tadeusz seemed to want to talk only to me. I felt flattered, yet even as we spoke, I had one eye observing: Greta flirting outrageously with Zygmus, imploring him to comb out some leaves that had lodged in her pretty curls; Tova, Josef, and Kuba singing a humorous Yiddish song; Irena and Sosia laughing hysterically about I don't know what; Janusz and Masha completely absorbed with each other in intense discussion.

"The main thing," Janusz told her, "is that we make our bodies strong so we'll be able to work the land. To me that's what Zionism is—a return to agriculture."

"I agree," Masha said, "but now the ultimate goal should be to leave—to *save* ourselves!"

The two talked so loudly that all the others stopped their own conversations and were drawn into theirs. I saw how the dream of a Jewish homeland—a country we could call our very own—had grabbed hold of everyone, though everyone's view of it was different. Opinions flew back and forth.

"We must," Janusz said passionately, "not merely create a society, but create a *just* society based on Jewish labor."

"Zionists should speak for *all* Jews in Poland, not just themselves!"

"Zionism can work only if we dedicate ourselves to equality between men and women!"

"Every Jewish girl should donate her jewelry to help buy land in Palestine!"

The discussion was passionate and bright. Only I had not contributed to it, so Tadeusz, to be polite, asked me what my thoughts were.

"Perhaps," I began cautiously, "we could work together to create a just society right here in Europe. Yes, even *here* in Poland. We could better our condition by working for economic and social justice through parliamentary means."

My words, parroted from Mother, were meant only for Tadeusz but, as there was a sudden lull in the conversation, were heard by all.

"Social justice here? Economic justice in Poland?" Masha hooted. "You sound like a socialist, but I don't think you are. I think you're just naive!"

Naive! My face reddened. How dare she call me naive!

"You can't *believe* what you just said, can you?" Masha continued, looking at me intently.

I didn't know exactly what I believed, but since all eyes were on me, I answered firmly, "Of course I do. I have faith that eventually life here for us will improve. After all, the rabbis themselves say we must have faith!"

"But, Lena," Greta said gently, "to believe that you can make your life better somewhere else—isn't that faith?"

I was thinking how to respond when Masha turned to me again and in her fearless voice said, "Lena, if you're a Jew and not a Zionist, you are without a country. You are homeless."

Homeless! What did she mean? Sometimes I *felt* as if I belonged to no country, but beyond these private feelings, wasn't I German? Of course I was! Masha's comment angered me. Homeless! What did *she* know about me? Nothing! Yet the silence of the others told me they agreed with her.

As the talk continued, the sun dropped low until it was almost submerged in the lake. I wanted to leave. I wanted to go home. I felt confused, nervous, tired. My heart was filled with strange emotions and I wanted to be alone. I stood up, grabbed my cake plate, and made an excuse to leave. After a round of good-byes, I slipped away into the birch grove, walking among the thin white trunks and rippling leaves. The soft earth underfoot and the leaf sounds gradually soothed me. What is happening? I wondered. Why do I feel so odd?

"May I walk with you?"

Startled, I turned to see Janusz standing a few feet behind me.

"Did you follow me?"

"Of course."

"Why?"

"Thought you looked a bit melancholy back there."

"I'm not melancholy!"

"Well, then you won't mind if I walk with you."

I felt like saying, "Why don't you walk with Masha?" but instead I said, "You're very kind, but I'd rather be alone."

I turned to walk on, but Janusz reached out and took hold of my arm. His grip was strong. He held me fast, turning me toward him. His eyes looked into my own and he said, "You don't like me, do you?"

Despite his boldness, his eyes and his voice told me he was vulnerable. Looking up at him, I was amazed again by his good looks. "I don't like your politics," I answered hastily, but then thought it sounded rather clever.

"Politics!" He laughed, letting go of my arm. "What politics?"

"Zionism—it's unpatriotic."

"Oh?" he said, amused. "Unpatriotic to whom? To Poland? Jews are not full citizens here, not even considered Poles, so how can I be unpatriotic?"

"I'm not speaking about you," I answered, "but *me*. I'm a German."

"Jews in Germany are no longer considered citizens either. Or aren't you aware of the new German sentiments?"

"I'm aware of everything. My brother is a reporter for the *Berliner Tageblatt*."

Janusz said nothing to this. He let go of my arm and we walked toward the town. Walking beside him in the glow of sunset, I could feel him looking at me, and I got that jittery feeling all over again.

"I think," he said cautiously, "it might be a good idea if you came to one of our meetings—you might change your mind."

I didn't answer right away, so he continued. "What I mean to say is I'd like to take you to one of our meetings sometime. I really would."

"I'm not interested."

"Masha is the president; she could tell you about our agriculture group—our goals. Masha . . ."

"I'M NOT INTERESTED IN WHAT MASHA HAS TO SAY!" I shouted, suddenly enraged by feelings I could not explain. "Don't you understand? *Germany* is my Fatherland. *Germany* is my homeland, not some desert in Palestine!"

Taken aback by my outburst, Janusz said nothing, but his face showed that he scorned what I said. His silence was fuel to some fire within me.

"In Berlin," I told him, "my brother sees evil everywhere yet has hope. He says the bad things in Germany are just for *now*. Reason will prevail, and soon everything will change."

"Yes," Janusz said. "Everything will change for the worse."

"I don't agree; I have faith."

"Faith is a liar."

"Why are you so cynical?" I cried. "I'm not talking of *waiting* faith but *working* faith. I'm talking about people who work against evil. People who oppose the Nazis every day. Right now there are people in Germany working hard to combat the hatred and violence of the Nazis."

"They'll all be shot."

He said this so matter-of-factly, his words sent fear into my heart as I thought of Günther. Suddenly I was angry with Janusz for making me afraid. I was furious!

"What do you know?" I cried. "Your dreams may be good for you but not for me. My father was a patriot who died for his country. My father is a German hero! Proud son of our Fatherland. A martyr! And as his daughter, I will not forsake our country!"

"Then why are you living in Poland?" Janusz asked, not even trying to suppress a smile.

His question unnerved me, for I could not come up with an answer. My mind was all muddled. And his smile—was he laughing at me? I felt humiliated! In fury I flung the cake plate at him, hurling it like a discus thrower. Fortunately he ducked and it sailed over his head, crashing against a tree, bursting into a hundred pieces.

Janusz stood silent, stunned by my rage. Then, seeing my confusion, he reached his hand out to me, but I turned and ran. He did not follow.

I ran all the way up the lakeside and rushed home. My heart hammering, I bolted up the stairs, entered my room, and slammed the door. I leaned my head back against its cool dark wood and gave way to tears, the words echoing loudly in my head: I hate him! I hate him! I hate him!

EIGHTEEN

DESIGN CONTEST

Can you design a beautiful dress for the new German Fräulein? Create the evening dress that best shows the new German spirit, and you could see your creation modeled by German cinema star Lotte Reinaur.

I read the contest rules again, then turned my eyes to the evening dress I had designed. I gazed at my drawing, trying to see it as one of the judges might, but it was impossible. I admired my entry too much. My confidence showed in the very words I wrote on the entry form to describe the dress:

For the elegant appearance that every German girl is now cultivating, my dress is cut on the bias and sewn in sections that hug the figure yet do not require fastenings. As you see, below the knees the dress flares in fullness diagonally to the ankles. The sleeveless V-neck bodice allows freedom of movement and is both simple and sophisticated. The fabric is ivory-colored silk of good weight. The smart sash at the hips is blue satin brocade in a Chinese stork design stitched with gold tinsel thread. I recommend pale silk stockings and gold-colored shoes with pyramid-shaped heels to accent the gown's Oriental allure.

I slipped the application and drawing into a large envelope and sealed it. Without telling a soul, I would mail it tomorrow. My design would be in the mail, and if I won, maybe I'd have a chance one day of going to the Schlechauer Fashion School in Berlin. Maybe.

All summer I dreamed of fashion school as I sewed for Pani Poyarska and helped Mother in the store. When I wasn't dreaming, I was dating. Before Tadeusz left for America, he and I spent a lot of time together. We saw films and took tea at Schenken's café. In our good room we read to each other, and sometimes I rode the bus with him to Wresnia, where I ate meals with his family.

We were not in love. Both Tadeusz and I dated other people. He went out with Masha, Irena, or Greta, and I went out with Rabbi Fried's nephew when he came to visit, and once with David, a young shoe salesman from Frankfurt. Sometimes too, we'd all go out as a group to sit in the café, or to visit in someone's home. Yet my social life was temporary, as everyone else was preparing to leave.

By early September only Masha, Janusz, Greta, and I remained. I was too envious to be friends with Masha and too embarrassed to speak to Janusz after the plate incident. Twice I saw them walking together, and I avoided them both. Then in mid-September Greta broke the news: She too was leaving! Her family was moving to Copenhagen, where her maternal grandparents lived. Greta threw herself into such a whirlwind of packing and studying Danish that I felt quite forgotten, yet I was happy for her, so I hid my sadness at the news. But the night before she left, when she came to say good-bye, we both cried like children.

"I'm sure you'll come visit me soon!" Greta declared to comfort us both.

After she left, I felt utterly alone. Greta had been the last link with my old group, and losing her made me feel like a sole shipwreck survivor.

Autumn of 1931 arrived. Coal wagons began their morning deliveries, twilight came early, bringing air tinged with chimney smoke, and on the Baltic wind dry leaves fluttered into our store. It was then I received the letter saying that I had not won the fashion design contest. My disappointment was great, but in this season our Holy Days veered us toward compassion, so I chose to think not of myself but of Mother.

Mother was a quiet person, but in the past year she had grown even quieter. Most of her friends had also moved away, and now her almost continual solitude frightened me. It seemed to me too that of late she was more than just steadfast; she had become uncompromising. I often avoided talking with her now, knowing that she was not merely preoccupied but obsessed with our store.

One evening I went downstairs to get an apple. The good room was dimly lit by a single lamp, and I saw Mother sitting on the velvet settee. In her hands was the little gray leather box holding Ta Ta's medal, yet she stared into the darkness.

I approached her. "Mother?" She did not answer. I sat beside her. "Mother, what are you thinking about?"

She continued to stare and, without turning to me, said in a barely audible voice, "Everything." I knew she was thinking of Ta Ta, so I sat beside her for a while, eating my apple. After I'd finished it, I heard myself say, "It's not a staying world. Things never stay, do they?"

"Love stays," Mother said.

"Always?"

"Always."

When she said this, I too thought of Ta Ta, for I knew that despite death, I would love him always. My love would *never* go away. I would love Ta Ta when I was forty and when I was seventy. As I had loved him in my fleeting child-years, I would love my father forever.

I wanted to ask Mother more about love, especially about the other kind of love—between a man and woman—but I didn't know what exactly to ask.

So pushing my questions back inside my heart, I asked instead, "Mother, are you all right?"

Snapping out of her contemplative mood, she said, "Of course I'm all right. Why shouldn't I be?"

"Because you're alone all the time. Because all you do is work and worry. Mother, you're still young, yet you live as if . . ." Here I paused at the words I was about to say, for they were unpleasant, but then said them quickly: "As if you're an old widow."

Rather than be offended, Mother laughed. "What would you have me do? Dress like Marlene Dietrich? Smoke cigarettes? Dance till dawn!"

"Why not? Why shouldn't you enjoy life? Somewhere there must be a nice gentleman, a widower just right for you."

"God help me!" Mother exclaimed. "I have too much on my mind to think of nice gentlemen!"

"You're worrying about the store, aren't you?"

Mother was silent, for my question brought her back to her problems. Then she answered dully, "Last month our profit was so small, I had to pay the Berlin shoe order from our savings. I don't know what we're going to do, because I don't know what's going to happen. . . ." Her voice trailed off in vagueness, but I knew what she meant.

Our town newspaper, *Lech*, had stepped up its campaign of *Swoj do swego!* urging the townspeople to shop only from Christian Polish stores. To shop from

Jews, the newspaper declared, was unpatriotic, so now every issue published a list of stores to avoid, ours among them. *Swoj do swego!* the newsprint screamed again and again. "Stick to your own kind!"

Despite the newspaper warnings, some of our more finicky customers stayed with us, but came only to the stockroom through the back entrance so as not to be seen. And there were those even more fearful, who telephoned us to deliver a pair of Katz shoes to their home—in a discreet bag. Worst of all, there were the many customers who boycotted our store completely, switching their allegiance to Wieski's Shoe Emporium. The result of the *Lech* campaign was dramatic. In the past months our sales had been cut in half.

I hadn't planned on telling Mother my great idea just yet, but now seemed the perfect time. "Mother, I know how we could make more money."

"Oh?"

I dropped my bombshell—drawing the words out slowly. "We'll sell our shoes at the market."

Mother looked at me as if I'd gone mad. "At the market? Katz Fine Shoes at a stall in the marketplace!"

"Listen, Mother, I've got it all worked out—"

"If our customers," Mother interrupted, "won't enter a Jewish store for fear of being seen, why would they buy from us at the market—in front of everyone!"

"Because they won't know they're buying from us."

"What are you talking about?"

"I'm talking about Pan and Pani Krieski selling our shoes at the marketplace—at their stall, in fact."

If Mother had thought I was crazy before, this suggestion confirmed it. "How can you even think such an idea!" she cried. "Pan and Pani Krieski are peasants who sell cheap shoes out of a potato crate!"

"That's why *our* shoes will be not only a novelty but a bargain!"

Mother said her next words very slowly and deliberately, as if reasoning with a small child. "Do you honestly believe that Pan and Pani Krieski would tolerate our competition?"

"Oh, we don't *compete* with them! We *unite* with them! We order the shoes; they sell the shoes. We assist them and split the profit!"

As Mother thought about this, I said, "Sure, we'll make less profit, but we'll sell more shoes."

"Perhaps," Mother admitted, "but Pan and Pani Krieski would be taking a risk selling shoes from a Jewish store openly in the market. They'd never agree."

"They already have."

"What are you saying?"

"I'm saying I asked them and they said yes."

An automobile horn sounded in the street, followed by the night tolling of the bells of Saint Adalbertus. Mother stared again into the darkness as if an answer to our broken life were hidden in the shadows. "It's a pity to see our lovely shoes sold from a crate, to see Katz quality service come to this."

"In a few months we won't have savings with

which to buy shoes. Then we'll have neither money nor shoes, nor a store. So perhaps, Mother," I said as gently as I could, "Katz quality service really doesn't matter anymore."

"We still have to keep the store open," Mother reasoned, "so how can we be here *and* in the marketplace? How can we be in two places at once?"

"You'll manage the store while I help Pan and Pani Krieski sell at the market."

In the dim lamplight Mother looked at me with a mixture of admiration and concern. I leaned over and kissed her petal-soft cheek. "Don't worry," I murmured. "I'll make it work."

———

By eight in the morning on Tuesdays the Ledniezno marketplace was abuzz. So many wagons jammed the town square, you had to weave about as if in a maze. And the noise! Truck horns honked rudely, making the horses rear. Pigs pulled by ropes around their necks squealed pitifully. And in hundreds of wooden cages on the ground were crammed chickens, screeching as if guessing their fate. Jewish women with thick Yiddish accents bargained for these chickens to take to the kosher slaughterer, and the vendors shouted at them to buy now! Why wait! At least give a look!

The Ledniezno market was a marvel. You could buy everything, it seemed. Gray salt and white salt, Danzig herring, buckets of broken eggs, goats, wigs, pigs, wheel grease, flypaper, new clothes, old clothes, live fish, buttons, and bulls. And the amusement of it!

The chickens frequently got loose, causing funny, noisy chases, the peasants tried on underwear over their clothes, and often a goat pulling a wagon of apples would be seen eating its own freight. Once a troupe of shabby actors borrowed crates from the onion seller and performed Shakespeare for coins. And another time the priest led a funeral procession right through the marketplace. Shaking a bell, he exhorted the crowds to kneel in prayer. And every Tuesday a weathered Gypsy woman stomped through the market holding a mangy parrot who, she shrieked in a parrot voice herself, would "tell your true fortune for two zlotys and without trickery!"

The stands of the shoe dealers crowded the eastern side of the marketplace. Here several long boards were set off the ground with bricks, and across the boards were slung shoes in pairs. A few shoe vendors, however, were more fancy. They displayed their shoes on top of wooden crates over which they had draped a piece of cloth. I stood at one of these makeshift display cases, that of Pan and Pani Krieski, and set out ten pairs of Katz Fine Shoes. Almost at once the shoes created a sensation. It was no wonder. The other shoes sold at the market were cheap, practical, and always black. But I purposely set out an array of imported American shoes. At first a few people stopped to just look at the shoes as if gazing at treasures in a museum. Then they became bolder, inspecting the shoes closely, marveling at the colors, feeling their fine leather, smelling them too. Even the barefoot peasants picked them up. I could see the appeal of these shoes was that they embodied a freedom of faraway America—flashy, modern, individual. The shoes were a hit. By the end of the day we'd sold every pair.

Working in our store meant the dismal tension of waiting for customers, making Mother and me depressed. But the market bustled with business, and I could almost pretend I was in the stream of Polish life. I would have enjoyed being at the marketplace had I not been so anxious about being discovered. The only thought that quieted this fear was that those customers who shopped for shoes at the market were not those who shopped in town, and this difference worked in my favor. Also, by wearing a big scarf tied under my chin and Mother's old coat, I blended in.

Yet one morning, just as I was setting out the shoes, I heard a familiar voice. "Lena, what on earth are you doing?" I looked up into Janusz's face. He was staring at me. I tried to compose myself, but my heart was pounding and I was painfully aware that in my disguise I looked frumpy.

"I'm selling shoes, of course!" I sang, trying to sound lighthearted. "What do you think I'm doing . . . washing pigs?"

Janusz did not smile, and his eyes bearing down on me made me blush and feel shaky. I remembered our last meeting, when I threw the cake plate at him. Why had I acted so childish? Still embarrassed at the memory, I looked down at nothing in particular, and there was a long awkward silence in which neither he nor I spoke.

"What are *you* doing here?" I asked at last, deflecting the attention away from me.

"Crossing the square to apply for my visa."

"Visa?"

"For Palestine. As Zionist leaders Masha and I might be given priority by the British government for entry visas, but we need to apply now—they take a long time to get."

He's going away, I thought . . . and with Masha!

An old woman stopped at the stall, and as I showed her the fine qualities of our shoes, Janusz did not leave. He stood at the side of the crates, watching me. Then, as soon as the woman left, he stood before me. He took both my hands, holding them solemnly as if they were holy things. "What are you doing here?" he asked gently.

Surprised by his tender gesture, my heart spun like a top and I gave out a forced laugh. "I told you. I'm selling shoes!"

"Why, Lena?"

"We need the money. Customers are not coming into our store—"

"Because of *Lech*?"

"Yes."

"But you put yourself in danger! A Jewish girl from town selling here openly—among a mob."

"I'm not afraid," I lied. "It's not what Mother and I like, of course, but it's what we have to do for now, for just a short while—until things get better."

Janusz said nothing, yet he held on to my hands.

Then, fearing someone might see us like this, I slipped my hands out of his and began dusting the shoes with a rag.

"I might be able to get you a visa too," he said quietly. "If you want one . . . if you would come with us."

I looked up from the shoes, and it was then, seeing his eyes, that I admitted to myself I was falling in love with him. I knew I could not stop the wild feeling that came upon me whenever he was near, the sense of sorrow and joy holding hands, possessing me, swooping me toward some unknown fate.

"We could," he said, "leave for Palestine together."

When he said this, I saw sunshine and palm trees and orange groves, and though I had never seen the seashore, in that moment I saw it, sky blue, and myself with tanned skin walking with him.

"Lena, you cannot stay here, for it will come to no good."

Why does he care? I wondered, and reasoned that he was probably pitying me. He is a good person, I thought, speaking only from compassion.

Two young women approached the stall, and just then Janusz bent close and whispered in my ear, "You must leave Poland, Lena. You *must*."

It was surprising how much that warm whisper in my ear felt like a kiss, yet tears filled my eyes and I had a sudden urge to weep. I looked down at the shoes on the crate top, the shoes that had become my whole life. Two tears fell like raindrops on the shoes, and

Janusz, seeing this, bent close. "Come with us," he urged tenderly. But he had said "with *us*," not "with *me*," and my broken heart understood his life was with Masha.

"Go away, Janusz," I said, turning from him. "Don't talk to me again," I begged. "Never!"

NINETEEN

I was determined to put Janusz out of my mind. I returned unopened a note he sent me, and once, when he came around to the house, I stayed quiet and did not answer the bell. I told myself again and again that though I was in love with him, he only meant to be a friend to me. Nothing more. During the day I kept myself so busy that I could easily push all thought of him into some dark recess of my mind. But at night, when I lay in bed without the sounds and colors of the world to distract me, in that dark, silent dreamtime I saw Janusz again in my mind and wept like the foolish girl I was.

I made myself concentrate only on selling our shoes at the marketplace, yet before even two months had passed, Pan and Pani Krieski announced, "It's too dangerous when we are seen with you; people are talking. We're in danger of having our stall closed down."

"I won't come to the market, but you could still sell Katz shoes," I told them. They handed me back the shoes. "Too dangerous."

I did not give up. That very day I got another idea: little hats made from broken umbrellas. I told Pani Poyarska to tell her customers not to throw away their damaged umbrellas but bring them to her, and she'd fashion a chic hat from the fabric. It was I who designed and sewed the hats, and they were so popular that I could have made 25 zlotys a week had not Pani Poyarska broken our relationship. "I'm so sorry," the kind woman said. "Too dangerous."

My failed money-making plans only made Mother more determined. "We have to succeed with the store," she kept telling me. "We must make a living through our *store!*"

I hated hearing Mother repeat this refrain, for it was increasingly difficult to stay in business, let alone thrive. We still had a few loyal customers. Not only Jewish families but Poles who were both kind and brave. Yet town censure and malicious gossip grew around them, and we knew their loyalty would not last. Like the others, they too would turn to Wieski's Shoe Emporium, and it irked Mother to no end that while we were nearly bankrupt, a man with such bad taste prospered. Mother was so angry about it that on Saturday, when we walked to synagogue, she made a point of crossing the street as we approached Pan

Wieski's Emporium. So it was a shock to us one early-December day when Pan Wieski himself walked into our store.

He seemed agitated about something, for as he caught his breath, his furry mustache twitched nervously. Pan Wieski was a stout, sluggish man, and now his snow-sprinkled fur coat and his cross face gave him the appearance of a bear roused from hibernation. For several moments he looked around but said nothing. Mother and I, frozen in surprise, said nothing either. Then, after making irritated swipes at his sleeves to brush off snow, he said in a gruff voice, "Pani . . . I mean *Frau* Katz, I have come to see you about an important matter."

"Oh, Pan Wieski?" Mother said, trying to appear calm. "What is that?"

"I'm sick to death of the filching woman!"

"The filching woman?" Mother asked.

"You know who I mean . . . the stealing woman. That sticky-fingered creature who creeps around the shops pilfering our merchandise. And has never been caught!"

Now Mother and I knew who Pan Wieski was ranting about. The filching woman, as he called her, was Pani Jablonska. She was not poor, yet over the past year she had made a habit of visiting shops and—while shopkeepers were distracted—stealing a blouse, a peach, a pair of stockings, a hairbrush, whatever she could easily take. She had stolen from us twice, once sneaking into the store while we were in the stockroom and leaving swiftly with a pair of satin slippers.

"That Jablonska woman pinched a pair of my finest pumps!" Pan Wieski fumed. "Artificial crocodile! She ought to have her hands cut off!"

Mother made a gesture toward one of our chairs, perhaps hoping that if Pan Wieski sat down, he'd also calm down. But Pan Wieski ignored her gesture. "I will no longer put up with thieves!" he announced as if to a great assembly.

I wondered what his not putting up with thieves had to do with *us*. But in the next moment Pan Wieski explained our connection.

"Frau Katz," he said, "you must come to court and testify with me against Pani Jablonska."

Mother replied, "I would like to help you, but I'm afraid I cannot."

"Why not?" Pan Wieski demanded.

"Well, we both know," Mother said, looking straight into his eyes, "testifying against Pani Jablonska in court would not be the best course of action. If we testify, they'll put her in jail, but she's a sick woman, not a criminal."

"If she's not a criminal then she's a kleptomaniac, and in either case she must be punished—put away where she can't harm honest businesspeople."

"I sympathize with what you say," Mother said pleasantly, "and I'm sure we can work out a solution to the problem."

"There is no solution but to take her to court and testify against her."

"I won't testify," Mother told him firmly.

"*Other* shopkeepers will testify," Pan Wieski said.

"They're free to do what they please," she answered, pretending to busy herself with a stack of invoices.

Pan Wieski walked to the counter where Mother stood. He came very close to her—too close, I thought. In a low, meaningful voice he said, "It would look very bad then if the only shopkeeper who didn't testify was the *Jewish* shopkeeper."

Unruffled, Mother countered fearlessly, "Are you threatening me, Pan Wieski?"

He ignored Mother's question. Pan Wieski had come for his own reason and was not to be deterred.

"Frau Katz, let's not argue. It's a shameful thing to let sin go unchecked. We should *all* speak out against stealing. After all, we Ledniezno businesspeople must support each other." I was pretending to dust the chairs, and when I heard Pan Wieski say this, I sneaked a look at Mother's face. I knew his comment inflamed her, since she knew he didn't care a pig's sneeze about us and was himself a thief to take our customers!

However, Mother's face was impassive and her manner indifferent. Seeing she wasn't going to respond, Pan Wieski grew silent too. "It is unfortunate," he said at last in a gentle sorrowful voice, "that the Jew so often collaborates with the criminal, yet both go unpunished." He stared at the imported German shoes in our window. He picked one up, a lady's wine leather pump with a delicate heel strap. "Feinstag's?" he asked.

Mother, now so angry, did not answer, so Pan

Wieski gave out a sigh. "I've never seen this style."

"It's new," replied Mother coldly.

"Lovely," Pan Wieski said. "Charming."

A week later my mother received a court summons to testify against Pani Jablonska. It was official. Pan Wieski had put forth Mother's name as a witness to Pani Jablonska's thievery. Now Mother had to testify, for if she refused, she'd bring suspicion on herself for protecting a criminal. But Mother refused and sent the summons back with this note: *Pani Jablonska is mentally ill. I cannot testify in court against her.*

We thought that was the end of it, but when Mother and I arrived at our store the following Monday, we saw a policeman pasting a large sign on our window.

NOTICE
BY ORDER OF THE LEDNIEZNO
CITY COUNCIL
KATZ FINE SHOES IS IN VIOLATION
OF CITY CODES.
THIS SHOP MUST REMAIN CLOSED FROM
5 DECEMBER TO 28 DECEMBER 1931.

Mother moved to unlock the shop door, but the policeman yanked her arm and shoved her aside.

"You are not to open the store!" he shouted.

"It's our store, so who are you to tell us what to do?" I cried.

My defiant manner to the policeman frightened

Mother. She pushed herself between the two of us. "Excuse me," she said. "We have operated our business here for years, so would you be so kind to tell us *why* our store is being closed?"

"Orders of the City Council," the policeman answered mechanically. "You have violated city business codes."

"Business codes?" Mother asked. "What codes?"

I didn't think the policeman would answer, but to my surprise he opened a small leather notebook from his jacket pocket and unfolded a written report of our alleged offenses:

1. Selling shoes to prostitutes.
2. Closing the store on Saturdays.
3. Speaking German while customers are in the store.

Standing on either side of the policeman, Mother and I read the offenses and noted at the bottom of the report a line saying the complaint had been filed by Pan Wieski.

Throughout the Christmas season our store was closed, and when it reopened, almost all our customers were too afraid to enter. To sell shoes we now were forced to wait for someone to telephone an order, and then we'd make a discreet home delivery.

One dark January afternoon Mother handed me a slip of paper with the name of a customer who had just telephoned.

"Who is Pan Dobrowski?" I asked grumpily. "I've never heard of him."

"Perhaps he's new in town," replied Mother. "He wants us to bring to his home a pair of men's fleece-lined slippers. Black, size forty-four."

Another coward, I thought angrily as I walked to the stockroom. I found the slippers, took them out of their box, and placed them in a plain bag not printed with our store name. I wrote out the receipt in advance, then took some money with which to make change. Tightly holding the paper on which the address was written, I went on my delivery.

The address was on a street thirty minutes away by foot. I walked fast, not only because it had started to rain, but because I wanted to get the offensive errand over with. Soon I came to a street of old but respectable apartments. Mother had written only the street number of the apartment building, yet each building had dozens of apartments and I hadn't the apartment number. How on earth would I find this customer?

As I stood in the rain wondering what to do, I spotted Milosz, the street sweeper. "Milosz!" I cried. "Do you know in which apartment Pan Dobrowski lives?" Milosz was simple as syrup, yet he knew nearly everyone and his memory for numbers was astonishing. Milosz leaned on his broom, grinning. "Fish weather, frog weather, frog frog frog! Frog weather, fish weather, frog weather! Fish frog fish!"

"Milosz! Do you know Pan Dobrowski, Milosz? Tell me, what apartment does he live in? Which number?"

Slowly Milosz stopped his singing and tried to make his mind work. "Pan Dobrowski . . . gave me a shirt."

The rain poured down. I felt my hair drip with cold water under my coat collar.

"Fish weather!" Milosz exclaimed joyfully, then, facing the sky, opened his mouth wide to catch the raindrops. As he was enjoying his "drink," I asked again, this time nearly shouting, "What is the *number* of the apartment where Pan Dobrowski lives? Tell me, tell me the number!" I begged.

Resuming his useless sweeping of the puddle-filled sidewalk, Milosz looked at me happily and sang in a kindergarten voice, "Number eighty-seven, little girl. Number eighty-seven, little girl."

I was so grateful I could have kissed his unshaven cheek, but instead I hurried to apartment 87, which I found up a long flight of concrete stairs. I rang the bell and with my soaking-wet hair waited anxiously. Hurry, Pan Dobrowski! I commanded silently. I don't want to catch pneumonia because of you!

I rang again, waited, then was about to leave when the door opened. But standing there was not Pan Do-browski. Standing there was Janusz.

"You're not Pan Dobrowski!" I blurted in shock.

"No, my grandfather is, but he's not home."

"I brought him the slippers," I said weakly, still reeling from the surprise.

"He doesn't want them," Janusz said.

I was so perplexed, I could only stand speechless with my wet hair plastered to my head.

"You see," Janusz explained in a great rush, "I ordered the slippers only to talk with you."

"*You* ordered the slippers?"

"Yes, and I'm sorry, truly sorry, if I caused you trouble. I know it was wrong of me, but you refused to speak to me, and well . . . I needed to talk with you. Alone."

I looked at him, not knowing what to think. He was deceitful to make me come all across town in the rain on a false pretense. A trick! That's what it was. A devious trick. He'd made a fool of me! I should have been angry. Insulted! I should have told him off for pulling such a selfish stunt! But I didn't.

I followed my heart and stepped inside.

TWENTY

"I wanted to see you," Janusz explained. "I wanted to talk with you." We were standing in a plain, book-lined room, where my coat was drying on a chair in front of a coal stove. The whole room smelled of damp wool.

"Why me?" I demanded. "Why did you want to see *me*?"

"Do you really want to know?"

"Yes."

"Because I think about you all the time."

I stared at him, too surprised to speak.

"Why do you look so stunned?" he asked. "Is it so hard to believe that you are on my mind? All the time."

"But," I stammered, "I thought you . . . I thought you and Masha—"

"Masha and I are friends," Janusz interrupted. "And we share a vision. But you, Lena . . . it's you with whom I have fallen in love."

He paused as I stood transfixed by his words; then he continued, "I love the funny way you speak Polish, the way you work so hard for your mother, the way you look down when you feel shy. I love the flash in your eyes when you smile. I love that you know Goethe. I love how you threw that big flowerpot. I love your laugh—like brook water. I loved the way you cleaned my cheek—your hands were so gentle. I love that you wear flour sacks. Actually *wear* them! I love your spirit even when you argue—like that day in the birch grove when you threw the plate."

Janusz spoke his words ardently and without guile. I was moved by his honest emotion, yet he had not said, "Your lips are a rosebud" or "Your eyes are stars."

Lena is plain . . . and it's kinder that we tell her now than let her get hurt when some boy tells her! Dora's long-ago words echoed in my head.

No, I thought. I'll tell him myself. And my words came out, "I'm not pretty."

"No, you're not pretty," he admitted, coming close to me. So close I could breathe in the clean, warm smell of his skin. I did not back away. "You're beautiful," he whispered. I didn't laugh at this, for in that moment I was. Right then. And in that moment he gently placed his hand under my chin and tilted my face toward his. He kissed me. We kissed. Our kiss was pillow soft—an explosion; lake smooth—fire!

Tante Ilse used to say that love turns one person into two and two into one. She was right. With Janusz I began to feel things not just with my heart, but with his too. Yet other times our spirits merged as if we were a solitary being, separate only from others.

We saw each other every afternoon. Despite the cold, we took walks together down to the lake, into the woods, to the windmill, to the tiny villages that lay beyond the town. We sometimes went to City Park, even to the Daisy Dell, where I told and retold my memories of Sala, and he smoothed the sharp-edged fragments of grief that wounded me still.

Being with Janusz was not dating. We didn't dance or go to parties. We rarely went to the cinema and never to Schenken's, as going to cafés now was too risky for Jews. But we visited a hundred places together in our minds, traveling back and forth to each other's thoughts like voyagers. We explored poems, scouting out meanings and prospecting for beauty as if for gold. We described our dreams, spoke of subjects much bigger than ourselves, and we laughed. In our grim lives we found humor. Telling jokes, we sought to make each other joyous, if only for a moment.

Love was something stronger than I could ever have imagined. Love was a force, lifting me from this troubled life into one where happiness teased. And this too was what love taught me—that life was neither happy nor sad but happy and sad blended. Threads of joy and of sorrow were stitched into life with the same needle and often in the same place. If I grieved over our store's failure, each day I rejoiced anew to see Janusz.

Janusz spoke often of his dream—the one he wanted to make *our* dream. He talked of a land edging the sea and planted all around with citrus trees. A land where we could be free. But his dream was distant to me. I kept it distant. I knew Janusz was planning to go to Palestine as soon as his visa was approved; he'd told me many times. Yet the words that fell from his lips seemed to me as extraneous as falling leaves. I kept my mind only on the present, our happy time together now. Perhaps my shortsightedness was due to love. Love had made me like an insect I had seen long ago in the Berlin museum. The insect was stilled, suspended forever in a beautiful, small piece of amber. And now I was frozen in this beautiful, brief time. Blissfully paralyzed.

But not Janusz. Everything about Janusz seemed not only in flux but on the verge of flight. His eyes searched a horizon I could not see, and as he spoke, his hands pushed the air as if it were in his way. His whole being yearned to leave, to flee, to fly. And when, each day before we parted, I lay my head in love against his chest, the sound I heard was a beating of wings.

TWENTY-ONE

February of 1932 was harsh. The snow did not just fall but swirled on a white wind that blasted through the streets like a siren. For several days Mother and I had not gone to our store, as the weather was too brutal even to make deliveries.

On one of these at-home mornings I threw on my coat and ran down to fetch the mail. Mother was preparing breakfast, and when I returned, I dumped the mail on the table and began sorting it: several bills, a letter from Tante Ilse, and to my surprise a letter from Janusz. Without comment I took his letter and stuck it in my coat pocket. But Mother, noticing, kissed my cheek. "You're an adult now," she murmured.

What did she mean by that? Her words made me blush. Flustered, I said, "Read Tante Ilse's letter." Using a knife, Mother opened the delicate paper and read aloud:

February 23, 1932

Dear Gisela,

I have not heard from you in a month and hope that you're well. I want to let you know that I am well despite the madness surrounding me. Yesterday Hitler announced at the Sports Palace that he'll run against Hindenburg for president! My heart races with fear. Hitler and that ugly Goebbels are already crisscrossing the country drumming up votes. Hitler shouts speeches all day, while Goebbels has posters put up and hands out pamphlets. Millions! My nerves are gone. The streets echo with the sound of loudspeakers blaring from the back of trucks. The Nazis have attached loudspeakers to gramophones playing records that announce "HITLER IS OUR LAST HOPE!" and "THE JEWS ARE OUR MISFORTUNE!" Nazis ride throughout Berlin blasting out evil lies with those damned loudspeakers. And huge crowds of people—may their mouths grow sores!—stop to cheer. The Tageblatt *says that about 3,000 Nazi meetings are held throughout Germany every day!*

So, dear sister, you will understand when I tell you that I have gone to the American Consulate, the Belgian Consulate, the Swedish Consulate,

*and a dozen more in the hopes that one will give
me a visa so I can leave.*

*Günther too should leave. What future can he
have here? I tell him he should leave, but he
doesn't want to, and besides he claims he's too
busy. He writes, writes, writes. But what can
words do?*

*Gisela, you don't have to deal with Nazis, but
think again why you are staying in Poland.
Think of Lena as well as yourself.*

Your loving sister,
Ilse

Mother read the letter in a soft breakfast voice, but
I noticed the pause she took after my aunt's suggestion that we not stay here. After Mother finished reading, I asked, "Well? What do you think of Tante Ilse's
advice?"

"It is easy to give advice."

"I suppose you mean," I pressed, "it's difficult to
take her advice—difficult to leave."

"Not just difficult, foolish. Running away solves
nothing. If you can't endure the bad, you won't live to
see the good."

"I didn't know life was an endurance test."

"What else is it then?" Mother asked. She stood up
and looked out the window.

I said cautiously, "I will want to leave Poland one
day."

Mother turned toward me. "You are an adult now.
You can do whatever you like—whatever is right for

you, Lena." Then she turned back toward the window. "The wind has died down; I am going to open the store."

"I'll come with you."

"No need. It's better you tend the house. You can make the noodle soup."

When Mother was gone, I walked slowly from room to room like a ghost. I felt as if I were floating, disconnected from everything. In the good room I stood in front of Ta Ta's photograph in its ornate gilt frame. I stared at it for a while. Then I blasphemed. In the dim room I lit one of our Shabbos candles and placed it on a table next to the Iron Cross and under Ta Ta's photograph—as if before an icon.

Then, kneeling as Christians do, I prayed. "Ta Ta," I begged, "help me. Help me know what is right! I am twenty now, yet so confused. I feel, Ta Ta, as frightened and foolish as the five-year-old you knew."

Knocking? Knocking. Someone was knocking at the door! I stood up, hastily put out the candle, then went to open the door. Janusz rushed in, his face red from the wind, his hair tousled and damp, and his coat bearing epaulets of snow.

"Take off your coat; I'll make some coffee," I said, moving toward the kitchen.

"No, don't. I can't stay long. I've come to tell you important news. *Wonderful* news."

"Tell me."

"I can leave Poland! I got a visa this morning from the British government to enter Palestine. Do you understand what this means? It means that I am one of a handful in the country who can leave. I'm assured of going!"

Shocked at the sudden news, I asked faintly, "When will you go?"

"Soon, and I want you to come with me."

Before I could respond, Janusz poured out his heart. His blue eyes sparkled with life and his whole face seemed to glow with hope. He spoke fervently in long, fast sentences, all connected, as if his very words were a train that could speed us away.

"You know the British are allowing only a small number of Jews to enter Palestine, but I've been given priority. The visas, Lena, are good for only one person unless that person is married—or engaged—then they're good for the couple. We'd need to leave by the first of March, so we can reach Palestine before the visa expires."

"The first of March? That's in a few days!" I cried.

"Yes, don't you see our luck? Without a visa we'd have to try to smuggle ourselves in. Now we can go easily. Freely! We'll take the train to Istanbul, then a boat to Haifa. We'll learn to work the land there, Lena. We'll learn to do anything so our children will grow up in sunshine."

"What about your architecture?" I asked.

He laughed. "One day I will design beautiful buildings and you'll design beautiful clothes. One day."

As he spoke, my heart was near bursting, yet everything was happening too fast, so I heard myself murmur, "I can't go on this trip with you."

My soft-spoken words fell on him like a blow. With

sudden anger he cried, "I'm not asking you to go on a *trip*! Don't you understand? This is not about a *trip* together; it's about a *life* together. It's about us—beginning a life. Beginning our life *together*."

"I understand," I pleaded. "I do understand, but . . ."

"You think you're not old enough!" he interrupted. "You think you need your mother's permission. You think maybe it's wiser to still try to get into some German fashion school! You think well, maybe someday, *someday* you'll go with me when you're not so afraid!"

His words, edged with scorn, met their mark, for there was truth in them. I *was* afraid. "I don't know whether it's right to run away," I stammered. "Surely, if we love each other, we can survive! After all, even where there's bad, there's also good. There's good everywhere, even here, and if there's not enough good, we can make some." I paused, for I was not sure what I was saying, nor even what I was feeling. At last, nearly in a whisper, I said, "Poland too is crowned with sacred shadows."

Janusz came toward me, tense and unbending. "You're right," he said. "There's good here too. But for us *here* and *now* there is more bad, and we've got a chance. We've got a chance others don't have. Lena, we must take it. We must!"

His words were seducing me, yet in fear I said weakly, "We have no money."

Janusz wrapped his arms around me. "We don't need money; we can make a life if we love each other." He turned my face up toward him so that we looked directly at each other. "We can make it, Lena."

His deep voice was firm yet also soft, caressing me. As so many times before, I laid my head against his chest. He stroked my hair, and I began to weep, for his words kissed my heart. The thought of being with only him from this day on seemed like a dream. Yet I was frightened of the unknown and so very unsure—not of him, nor of his love, but of *me*. Unsure of my duty to Mother—and to myself.

He hugged me hard. His breath was warm, his arms a cloak, his whole body my shelter. He hugged me as if he'd never let me go. As if *he* would never go.

"Lena, I love you!" he said, his voice almost a cry. "I want to be with you, no one else. I'm meant to be with you . . . as you're meant to be with me. We both know it!"

"I know . . . but it's all happening too fast!" I wailed in anguish. My mind raced, and my body felt again weirdly disconnected from me, as if floating in space. How, I thought, can I make him understand that things were happening too *fast*? How can I tell him that right now I feel childlike and helpless, unable to think clearly, unable to act? . . .

Janusz let go of me. He stepped back, his face grim. "You don't want to come with me."

"I can't!" I sobbed.

Through a blur of tears I saw his face as an image in a broken mirror, sorrowful, fragmented. He lingered for a moment, then turned, went to the door, and left.

And that is how on the morning of the twenty-sixth of February 1932, Janusz walked out of my life.

TWENTY-TWO

I tried to keep my mind on the store in the hope of forgetting Janusz. But the more I tried to ignore the pain, the more I hurt. At times I yearned to confess my grief to Mother. I longed to ask her advice and receive her comfort. But my heart sorrow was so intense, I could not speak of it.

Four days after Janusz left our house, the day after he left for Palestine, I was in the store totaling up the bills while Mother was taking inventory. It was early morning and there were no customers in the store. The photographer stationed in front of our shop ensured that no one would dare step in. This photographer, a young man from *Lech*, showed up often now and stayed for hours. His "job" was to take pictures of anyone entering a Jewish store. The next day the customer's photograph would be printed in *Lech* rimmed by a black border, as if it were a death notice, and the caption would always read: THIS IS A TRAITOR, A POLE WHO PREFERS TO SHOP FROM JEWS. Our customer's disgrace would serve as a warning to anyone else who might be tempted to buy from Jews.

We had three types of customers now: the ones we secretly let in the back door, the ones who requested discreet home deliveries, and the few who boldly came through the front door, photographer or not.

As I worked, Mother came out of the stockroom. From her resolute face I could see she had an idea. "Lena, before you came in this morning, Frau Gerhardt's maid telephoned."

"Oh?" I said, without the slightest interest.

"Frau Gerhardt would like a size thirty-two pair of silk Schoen evening shoes in light blue."

"Schoen shoes need to be ordered from Feinstag's," I said, "and you know Feinstag's will no longer sell to us. So I hope you told the maid to tell Frau Gerhardt to forget it. Tell her to go to Poznań or Danzig or Berlin. Tell her to go to Paris or better yet—hell."

Mother, ignoring my talk, said quietly, "I have the shoes for her."

"Impossible," I replied.

Then Mother reached into a bag she was carrying and pulled out a Schoen box, an old one. Inside the box was indeed a pair of very pale blue Schoen evening shoes.

"Where did you get those?" I cried.

"They're sample shoes; we've had them for a while."

"How long?"

"Six years."

"Six years!" I exclaimed. "You can't sell Frau Gerhardt sample shoes! And certainly not ones that have been around for six years! She'll see they're old right away! She'll see they're really dark blue shoes that have faded to light blue from being in the window so long!"

"She will like them," Mother said.

I was about to protest when she added, "As a wealthy lady of style and refinement, Frau Gerhardt recognizes quality, and others will follow her example."

I didn't know what Mother was getting at, but I began to feel uneasy. "What are you saying?"

"I am saying that if Frau Gerhardt were to decide to come to our store, to enter a Jewish store, to be seen in Katz Fine Shoes . . . if such a one as Frau Gerhardt were brave enough to do this, others might follow. Her patronage, her visible patronage would be an example for others."

"There's a great flaw in your argument," I countered angrily. "Frau Gerhardt is not a Pole; she's a German. Why would Poles look to *her* as an example?"

"She has money and style. They will."

"Mother, your reasoning makes no sense! I doubt her coming into our store would influence anyone. Besides, I can tell you right now Frau Gerhardt will *never* enter our shop. Never! Never! Never! Can you imagine selfish Frau Gerhardt risking public reproach?

Being slandered by *Lech*? Why should Frau Gerhardt enter our store if no one else will?"

"Because you and Dora were best friends."

If I had thought Mother off track, now I saw she was completely derailed. "That was a long time ago!" I said. "Dora and I don't even speak to each other. We haven't in years, ever since—"

"Old bonds, though not visible, can still be strong," Mother interrupted, her voice steady and persuasive. I looked at her with pity, for I saw that her strength came not from conviction but desperation. This was a wretched, foolish tactic to save her store, and I despised it.

"I want you to take the shoes to Frau Gerhardt and ask her if next time she would please honor us with a visit to our store, where she would be able to choose from a large selection."

"I won't do it," I cried. "I will never beg from Frau Gerhardt and I will not lie either. Large selection! We can't even sell her the shoes she wants! She'll see quick as a cat that the shoes are six years old!"

"Stop shouting, Lena. You can try."

"I DON'T WANT TO TRY!"

Then there was silence in which Mother and I just looked at each other, as if across an abyss. At last I said, "Besides, I would have no words to say."

Mother pulled out the small leather box. "I have thought of that," she said calmly. "This is what you will say. . . ."

I felt the keen humiliation of what Mother had asked me to do, yet as she told me the words, I saw not my mother but a stubborn, aging war widow with little money and little hope, and I agreed to do it. I even tried to make myself believe the approach made sense. Perhaps I agreed because deep within me I wanted to believe that just maybe, she might be right.

Mother wrapped the shoes in multiple layers of new pink tissue paper and placed them in a paper bag not printed with our store name. I opened the door of our shoe store and looked far down the street. No photographer. Good. Clutching the parcel tightly, I stepped out. The air felt blade sharp, as it does just before a snowfall. I walked quickly, rehearsing my speech to Frau Gerhardt.

TWENTY-THREE

"What size are these?"

"Thirty-two. Exactly what you asked for."

Frau Gerhardt looked at the shoes for a long moment, and I knew she fancied them. Perhaps it is now, I thought, that I should say the words to her. The words I promised Mother I would say. I reached into the pocket of my coat and withdrew the little box. For I wanted to believe that when Frau Gerhardt, who had once liked me, would hear my words and see, actually *see* what was in the little box, she would change back again. She would understand and be good to Mother and me again. Yes, I wanted to believe that what was in the little box had this power.

I opened the box to show her the Iron Cross, and my

words came out in a great passionate rush. "Frau Gerhardt, my mother and I have always respected the patriotism your family has shown for our Fatherland. We belong to a handful of Germans who are in a particularly difficult position, living here in Poland, outside our own beloved country. Yet we are faithful to, and proud of, our heritage. This venerated medal, Frau Gerhardt, is the highest German military honor and was given to my father for sacrificing his life for Germany. *Our* nation. Mother and I cannot expect that a distinguished recipient of the Iron Cross will be treated with respect by Poles, but surely by his fellow Germans! Frau Gerhardt, Mother and I are having a difficult time now, and so if you, in solidarity and respect to our Fatherland, would come into our lovely store, you would not only be able to choose from a wide selection of fashionable shoes, your support would show that—"

"How much are the shoes?" Frau Gerhardt interrupted.

"Pardon me, Frau Gerhardt?"

"I said, how much are the shoes? How much do you want for them? Forty-five zlotys?"

I looked up at Frau Gerhardt. Her face was still as a portrait.

Not waiting for my answer nor acknowledging anything I had said, she went to her handbag resting on a small chair. She pulled out some banknotes. "Well, why don't you answer?" she asked sharply.

I looked at her and now, after all these years, I saw her without beauty and without influence. I saw her as no more than a small, selfish woman. "They're free," I said, surprising myself. "You don't owe us a thing!" I shoved the little box into my pocket and rushed angrily from the room, down the stairs of the big house, and out into the street.

"Lena! Lena!"

I stopped and turned around. It was Dora. A tall young man in a brown uniform was holding her hand as she stepped out of a motorcar. I had neither seen nor spoken to her in four years. Despite my anger I stood transfixed as she rushed up to me.

"Lena!" she cried, the old gaiety in her voice. "Lena, I haven't seen you for ages!"

"Hello, Dora," I said indifferently.

Dora laughed her musical laugh, then turned her face up lovingly to the handsome soldier who stood by her side. "Hans, this is my old friend, Lena."

Hans clicked his heels and bowed. I stared at them both. Dora had grown even more beautiful. A beautiful, dark-haired woman. And she was wearing mink! A black mink coat with an elegant black mink hat that made her fair skin look fine as porcelain.

"Hans, darling, Lena and I used to play together when we were little girls."

"I bet you were a cute little girl," he cooed to her.

Dora smiled up at him, and as she did, I looked at her with both sadness and wonder. Dora slipped her hands out of her mink muff. "Look, Lena, Hans and I are engaged."

On Dora's left hand a large diamond ring sparkled in the cold morning light. Why she was suddenly so friendly to me I had no idea, but I suspected it was only to create a little performance for her fiancé. So I glanced apathetically at the ring and would have walked on had I not noticed it—the ring on Dora's other hand.

"You bought yourself another sapphire ring," I commented coldly.

She looked confused for a second, then laughed. "Oh, *this*! It's just my old sapphire ring. Imagine, Lena, when we had the piano tuned, we found it stuck inside the strings, right on F-sharp! Can you imagine! For weeks I couldn't figure out why every time I played that note, it sounded funny! So we fixed the piano and found my ring in the same moment! Wasn't I lucky?"

She was talking to me but looking up coquettishly at Hans. "You're a lucky girl all around," he teased.

The horror of her words caused me such pain, I was speechless. I turned from them and hurried away. I walked as if propelled, but in no particular direction. I walked all through the town. I don't know what possessed me, but I couldn't stop. I just kept walking as if I could walk off the pain.

I walked until I found myself at the bank of Lake Lipówka, and there I went toward the water, where a few pieces of ice floated like little islands on the surface. The bank was muddy and my boots were covered with slime, but I didn't care. I stood staring at the water. Listening to the silence.

Then I came closer to the water's edge, even stepping into the water a bit. I gazed at my dim, wintry reflection in the lake, and like another moment many years ago, I saw my own face merge with Sala's. How easy it would be, I thought, to stop all the hurt. How easy to slip under the cold water into that hushed stillness. Like slipping under cool sheets at nighttime.

I stood there for a long time, feeling I was in a dream. Feeling I could enter the other side of time. But at last the feeling vanished, and I turned from the lake. I had forgotten to wear gloves, so I shoved my hands into my coat pockets for warmth. At once my right hand felt the box holding Ta Ta's German medal. I hated the Iron Cross now with all my heart. It was a gaudy, worthless piece of metal. I took it out and thought of flinging it deep into the water. But I didn't. I remembered it was not mine but Mother's, and so I slipped the box back into my other pocket. When I did, I felt paper. Paper? I pulled it out—the letter from Janusz! Unopened. Forgotten. With near-frozen fingers I tore open the envelope and read:

Do you know the land where the lemon trees flower,
Golden oranges glow in the dark-leaved bower,
Where a gentle wind blows from an azure sky,
Unruffled the myrtle grows and the laurels rise high—
Do you know the land?
There, only there
With you, my beloved, I long to go. . . .

TWENTY-FOUR

The words were Goethe's, the love was Janusz's. In clinging to my life with Mother, I clung to childish helplessness, disobeying what Mother herself had once told me: "Listen to your heart." Well, I thought bitterly, it's too late to listen to my heart *now*. Janusz was gone. Sailing far away to a new life I would never share.

I gave way to sobs that racked my whole body and echoed eerily against the naked trees. I felt in those moments I could cry forever, but at long last I shoved the letter back into my pocket and began walking up the bank toward town. I went along the same path through the trees that Janusz and I had walked after the picnic. The cold air bit my wet cheeks. I headed back to our store by way of Kościuszko Street, which was now filled with morning business. Soldiers taking breakfast in steam-filled cafés, the blind beggar ringing his iron bell, housewives bustling with their market baskets, and the newsboy whose shrill shouting seemed at once innocent and depraved.

"MARCH 1, HITLER RAPIDLY GAINING SUPPORT!
MARCH 1, HITLER RAPIDLY GAINING SUPPORT!
MARCH 1, HITLER RAPIDLY GAINING SUPPORT!"

I hurried past him, wanting to rush far from his yelling, to stop hearing his news. But even at the end of the street I could hear the cry:

"MARCH 1, HITLER RAPIDLY GAINING SUPPORT!"

I put my hands to my ears to blank out the sound, and as I did, a thought curled its way into my mind, and I turned and hurried back toward the newsboy. Without thinking, I grabbed the paper right out of his hand and confirmed it. Today, the first of March! *Today!* The boy grabbed his paper back. I walked down the street again, struggling to make my mind work. "We'd need to leave by the first of March," Janusz had said. But how could *today* be the first of March? Wasn't the first of March *yesterday?* Like unschooled peasants at the market who figure prices with their hands, I counted on my fingers the days forward from the 26th of February, the last day I saw Janusz. I counted again and again but still, it made no sense. If this is the fourth day since the 26th, then today must be the *second* of March, not the first. I puzzled over this for several minutes until suddenly I remembered—1932. Leap year. Today is the first of March and that means he's leaving *today*, and perhaps, just maybe . . . he hasn't left yet! I ran toward his apartment. I raced so fast, I skidded on the icy street, regained my balance, and rushed toward his home like the crazed woman I was. I ran all through the town as wildly as I had done when I was five. When I reached his apartment, I flew up the stairs as if on wings, rang the bell, then knocked loudly on the door. No one answered. I waited a moment, then knocked again and again. I waited. I rang the bell. I knocked again on the door. I banged on it.

No answer . . . he had already gone.

I walked down the stairs and out into the street. I walked slowly, not caring even to wipe away my tears.

"Number eighty-seven, little girl!"

I turned to see Milosz behind me. He was propping his old bicycle up against a lamppost. Grinning shyly, he lifted his knitted hat and bowed. Had my heart been joyous, I would have smiled, for he was dear and his hair had been cut in a curiously funny, thick chunk and looked as if thatched.

"Hello, Milosz," I said dully as he took the scraggly broom off his bike and began to sweep. I watched him for a moment, then got an idea. "Milosz," I asked very slowly, "have you seen Janusz today? You know Janusz, Pan Dobrowski's grandson. Did you see him today?"

"Janusz," Milosz sang softly, "has gone far away."

"When, Milosz, *when* did he go?"

"He gave me five zlotys." Milosz began to dig in his pocket to show me the coins.

"Yes, but when did he leave, what *time* did he go?" At the word *time*, Milosz looked confused. I tried another tack.

"Is he coming back? Do you think Janusz will return here today?"

"No," he answered without thinking about it.

I stood beside him as he swept, then asked, pointing in the direction of the station, "Did he walk *this* way?"

"Train goes far away, far away."

"When?" My voice was thin glass.

Milosz did not answer.

I thought for a moment.

"Noon. Have to be at station by noon, noon, noon."

I stared at Milosz. Noon! That's it! Janusz would be taking the eastbound noon train. I looked at my watch. Eleven-thirty!

"I've got to get to the station!" I cried.

But how? The station was too far to walk—it'd take at least a half hour. A small bus went regularly from the post office on Kościuszko Street, but it was slow and sometimes there was unpleasantness for Jews trying to board it. I felt a tug on my arm. Milosz was pulling me toward his bicycle. He wanted me to take it.

"I can't!" I wailed. "I don't know how!"

Then, to my amazement, Milosz laid his broom across the handlebars and motioned for me to sit there—above the handlebars! It seemed to me impossibly difficult, like some circus trick, yet my desire to get to the station was so strong that, without thought to the danger and with Milosz's help, I hoisted myself atop the broom across the handlebars. Milosz raised himself onto the seat, and after a frightening, wobbly start we gained momentum and were off.

Milosz pedaled steadily at a good speed. I would normally have been terrified to be balanced like a book bag on a dilapidated bicycle and steered across cobblestone streets by a simpleton. But now I was singleminded. All my being focused on getting to the station, and I didn't care a zloty for my safety or that I looked like Milosz's wife sitting on that broom.

Down Zamenhof Street, down Brodsky Street, cross Kościuszko Street, one more corner, no—no, *two* more. Take the corners easy! Slow a bit . . . just a bit. That's it!

"GRUMPY FAT BEAR WITH COAT SO FURRY!" Milosz suddenly sang. We had just rounded the corner of Kościuszko Street, and there was Pan Wieski walking to his store. He stopped in his tracks to stare, shock-faced at our stunt.

"GRUMPY FAT BEAR WITH COAT SO FURRY!" Milosz sang this bit of jump-rope song again. We both laughed like fools, and then, not knowing what possessed me, I too sang at Pan Wieski as we passed him. Sang at the top of my lungs:

"GRUMPY FAT BEAR
 WITH COAT SO FURRY!

YOU SNORE ALL WINTER,
YET NOW YOU HURRY!
YOUR BELLY'S RUMBLING,
YOUR LEGS WOBBLING—
WHAT IS IT
YOU'LL SOON BE GOBBLING?"

"FISH!" shouted Milosz, tipping his hat to Pan Wieski, and we both chanted, "FISH! FISH! FISH! FISH! FISH! FISH! FISH!" Then at Pan Wieski's shocked face we laughed insolently, vanishing around the next corner like two imps from the netherworld.

"Don't slow down!" I cried. "Fast! Faster, yes, almost there! Faster! There! The brick stationhouse, I can see it now! Yes!

"Stop!"

Milosz slowed to a stop and I leaped off the bike, twisting my ankle as I did. I let out a yelp of pain, but seeing Milosz's concerned look, I gave him a kiss on his cheek, then limped off to find Janusz.

The train station was as busy as an anthill. Wagons were lined up right on the platform to convey the unloading freight from the train cars. Jumping atop and around these wagons were dozens of "back porters," the very poorest of Jews who had come up from the villages to find work. Though young, they ran bent over like old men as they carried loads of coal, wood, and potatoes on their backs. Some of the back porters pushed carts; others were harnessed to carts and pulled them like horses. Around the great hustle of the porters rose the bustle of the passengers running to buy tickets, catch trains, and shout good-byes. I looked at my watch. Ten minutes to twelve! I have to find Janusz! I made my way through the crowds on the platform, searching desperately for the one person I yearned to see. Yet I could not rush, for my ankle pain was great and the platform so mobbed that it was all I could do to keep from stumbling or being pushed over. I headed toward the ticket office, but every man I saw seemed to be Janusz. The back of a young man, the arm of another, the distant profile of yet another. Everywhere I looked, I saw Janusz and yet could not find him.

"Janusz!" I cried to no one, like a child lost from its parent.

No one answered.

"Janusz! Janusz! Janusz!"

With all my energy, I shoved aggressively through the crowd. In the distance I thought I saw him! But when the stranger turned and I saw his face, I gave out a wail as if I'd seen Satan himself. I backed away and turned to circle the whole platform one more time. I caught a glimpse of another young man emerging from the ticket office. Walking away—*away* from the station? I shoved again through the crowd, invoking expletives from people I had unthinkingly pushed.

He turned and walked faster. I *limped* faster. I cried his name. He didn't stop. I called again. He kept walking. I forged ahead. He moved on. I cried out again. Turning, he did not hear me. He could not hear me! He moved out of sight. A train pulled in, blasting its whistle, screeching its brakes, screaming in pain for me. In one last desperate push I propelled myself forward. There he was again! But was that really *him* in the distance? I stumbled forward, my arm extended in front of me like a beggar. My chest ached, my head throbbed. After one long, leaping limp, my fingers gripped the young man's shoulder from behind. He turned around.

It was Janusz.

"Lena!"

"I want to go with you!" I gasped. "I want to go with you!"

Janusz stared at me, speechless.

Though my heart burst with passion, I uttered only one more word: "Always."

Janusz wrapped his arms around me. "The train leaves this evening, but we must get your ticket before noon."

"I'll need to tell Mother."

"We'll tell her *together*," he murmured.

It began to snow. In the white air, Janusz and I kissed, sharing a single soul. Then we turned and walked across the muddy station yard toward the ticket office. As we went, I rested my head on his chest. The sky was cold and the wind cruel, yet my heart was warmed as if by fire. And the beating of wings I felt was my own.

AFTERWORD

Throughout 1932 five runoff elections were held in Germany to determine who would rule the country, the aging war hero General Paul von Hindenburg or the Nazi leader, Adolf Hitler. Though Hitler never received a majority vote, through devious political maneuvering he came to power in January 1933.

As soon as the Nazis seized control, they began the systematic persecution of the Jews. As a result of thirteen years of anti-Semitic propaganda, the Nazis had succeeded in making anti-Semitism appear respectable and patriotic. Opponents were intimidated into silence, or murdered. A wave of organized brutality swept over Germany. The Nazis evicted Jews from all public places: theaters, concert halls, museums, and parks. Jews were forbidden to have any social contact with Gentiles. In April 1935 all Jewish children were expelled from German schools, and by September the infamous Nuremberg Laws were passed. These two laws deprived Jews of all civil and legal rights. The first was The Reich Citizenship Law, which said that because of their impure blood, Jews were no longer German citizens, but considered only subjects. The second was The Law for the Protection of German Blood and Honor, which forbade marriage or employment between Jews and Gentiles.

Meanwhile in Poland, Marshal Pilsudski died—in 1935—and Polish anti-Semitism burst aflame. Jews were beaten on the streets and their homes were broken into. They were expelled from their jobs and from universities. Throughout Poland, Jews were degraded, imprisoned, and even murdered.

The Polish National Party greatly admired Hitler, especially for the ease with which he deprived political rights to German Jews—the most prosperous Jewish community in Europe. In 1937 Poland signed a non-aggression pact with Germany. This meant that Germany promised never to invade Poland. With this promise, the Poles could now openly support Hitler as they no longer feared German invasion.

Yet they were tricked.

In September of 1939 the Nazis invaded Poland, incorporating it into the German Reich. Once again Polish independence was lost.

Because of its large number of Jews and its strong anti-Semitism, Eastern Europe was the arena chosen by the Nazis for the accomplishment of their major goal: the extermination of all Jews. As soon as they conquered Poland, the Germans ordered the Jews deported to Warsaw and other large cities, where they were confined to ghettos. While thousands died in these ghettos of disease and starvation, the Nazis set up a network of concentration camps, the major ones in Poland, to which they ultimately brought Jews from all over Europe to be killed.

Six million Jews were murdered. In Poland alone the Germans killed nearly three and a half million Jews—including 75 percent of Poland's Jewish population.

After the war ended in 1945, many who survived the Holocaust wanted to settle in Palestine, which was then under British rule. However, thousands of survivors who arrived in Palestine were turned back by the British. At last, in 1948 the United Nations voted to make part of Palestine an independent Jewish homeland and in May of that year, the state of Israel was born.